THE
HEDGE
WITCH

BY CARI THOMAS

Threadneedle

THE
HEDGE
WITCH

CARI THOMAS

HARPER
Voyager

Harper*Voyager*
An imprint of HarperCollins*Publishers* Ltd
1 London Bridge Street
London SE1 9GF

www.harpercollins.co.uk

HarperCollins*Publishers*
Macken House, 39/40 Mayor Street Upper
Dublin1, D01 C9W8, Ireland

First published by HarperCollins*Publishers* 2022
2

A catalogue record for this book is available from the British Library

ISBN: 978-0-00-854670-0

This novel is entirely a work of fiction.
The names, characters and incidents portrayed in it are
the work of the author's imagination. Any resemblance to
actual persons, living or dead, events or localities is
entirely coincidental.

Set in Meridien by Palimpsest Book Production Ltd, Falkirk, Stirlingshire

Printed and bound in the UK using 100% Renewable Electricity by CPI Group (UK) Ltd

MIX
Paper | Supporting
responsible forestry
FSC™ C007454

This book is produced from independently certified FSC™ paper
to ensure responsible forest management.

For more information visit: www.harpercollins.co.uk/green

To the magic of Wales and my uncle Roger Couhig,
a Welsh wizard, storyteller and dreamer.

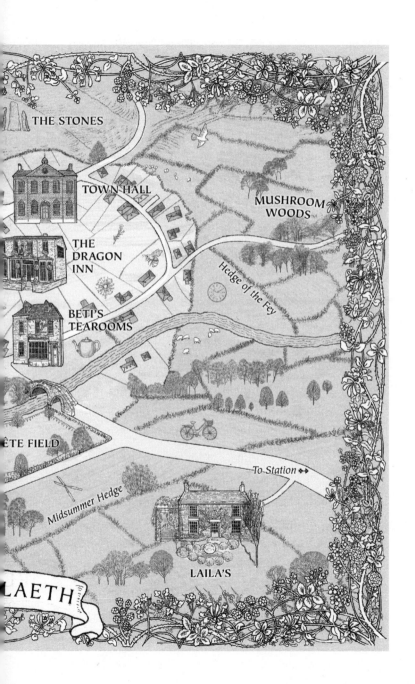

THE STONES

TOWN HALL

MUSHROOM WOODS

THE DRAGON INN

Hedge of the Fey

BETI'S TEAROOMS

FÊTE FIELD

To Station

Midsummer Hedge

LAILA'S

LAETH

I call to the watchtowers of the East!
To the Goddess of Air and Wind,
Wielding the wand of old.
To the leaves in the sky,
To the birds flying high,
To the scents of the flowers,
To limitless powers.
To the wisest of minds,
And the freest of souls,
Rise now and let your story go.

WHEN TIME MELTED

Rowan breathed onto the train window. A circle of mist appeared, soft as the blur of the landscape beyond. She drew two eyes and a smile inside it. Then, with a small burst of magic, the smile turned itself upside down. She glanced up and down the carriage – but no one was around to see her cast. It was empty. After all, why would anybody be going to a small, desolate village in mid-Wales on a perfectly good Saturday?

Anyone but me. Why me?

Exiled for the summer! Cast out! Left to fend for herself amid the sheep and bogs!

She could be going on holiday somewhere hot, with a beach. She could have stayed in London and attempted to attend parties she hadn't been invited to. Even band camp was a preferable alternative. There were boys at band camp. But no. She'd been packed off for the summer to reside with Aunt Winifred, her arguably most crazy relation – and there was stiff competition. What chance would she have now when she returned to St Olave's School for Girls having missed the entire summer's social scene? Rowan laughed aloud. She wasn't exactly *in* the social scene . . . but now she was as far from it as you could get, hurtling on a train towards the middle of nowhere. It was like facing her future – one day she'd probably *be* Aunt Winifred, living in a remote cottage surrounded by cats, smelling of cats, turning slowly but surely doolally, poking a stick at the local children if they came near.

Rowan sat back in her seat despairing at the vision. She'd hoped for a very different summer. Free of the chains of school, of the people who made it clear she would never be one of them, perhaps she'd find friends – friends who didn't think she was a joke. Maybe she'd meet someone. Have a fling. It was necessary – she'd be going into the Sixth Form next year. Everyone at school had started coupling up, growing up, and she felt as if she were being left behind. No one ever looked at her with *that* kind of interest. *Who would want me?* Rowan batted the thought away, preferring her hyperbolic despair.

Just one kiss! One spectacular, spell-shattering kiss! Was it too much to ask of the Goddess? Or would she be alone forever? Never been kissed. It would be written on her gravestone:

Here Lies Rowan Greenfinch: Sorely Missed But Never Kissed. Buried With Cats.

A trundle of wheels distracted her before she could begin writing the full extent of her bleak obituary in her head. A young woman pulled up a tired-looking food trolley next to her. 'Do you want anything?' she asked, rolling gum around her mouth.

'A boyfriend?' Rowan suggested.

The woman stopped chewing, eyebrows meeting in confusion. 'Wha—?'

Rowan laughed. 'Sorry. Sometimes I say things out loud that are meant to be in my head. But hey, if you can't do me a boyfriend then I guess I'll take my own body weight in chocolate. Have you got that in there?'

The woman stared at her. She looked concerned. 'I've got Cadbury's Dairy Milk or KitKats. Do you want . . . all of them?'

Rowan sensed her humour was lost on her. 'I'll take a KitKat. Just the one.' She didn't want a KitKat but felt it was the least she could do now she'd confounded the poor woman.

'Sure.' The woman appeared relieved the exchange was over. The trolley trundled on through the empty carriage, rattling despairingly.

Rowan took out a bag from beneath her seat – the bag of treats her mum had packed for her. She threw the KitKat inside and breathed within – it was like opening up an oven with a freshly baked cake rising inside. Warm garden herbs and molten sugar. It smelled like home. Rowan didn't know how many baked treasures the bag contained altogether, probably a six-month supply, knowing her mum. She could see lavender cookies, vervain brownies, nettle seed nut bars—

She picked out a marigold madeleine, a Bertie special. She bit into it, the marigold butter melting over her tongue and coaxing a smile to her lips. It was impossible not to smile when her mum's marigolds were involved. Bertie had once served them at a wake, which had made for an awkward end to the funeral, everybody beaming away while they remembered the loss of Great-Granny Iris.

Rowan chuckled at the memory and settled back into her seat, surrendering to the view beyond the window, admitting that it *was* beautiful. Unearthly beautiful. The train poured through the middle of a valley, green hills peeling away on either side, rising slowly to larger, stony mountains, their rough, torn edges distressed with cloud; so many types of light that Rowan could hardly take them all in: thick golden curls high in the sky, rain-dusted beams piercing the clouds, rivers of light carving the textures of the mountains and falling windswept across the fields, restless and wandering, disappearing into dark knots of woods and finding silver stillness on the surface of sudden lakes. It was like something from a fairy tale. Wild, mythical, and . . . desolate.

Rowan's phone went off, breaking the enchantment. She untangled it from her pocket. It was her mum. It was always her mum. She answered the call and Bertie's voice was direct. 'Are you on the train?'

'Mum, you literally put me on the train.'

'Well, are you still on it? You haven't fallen off? Or been kidnapped?'

'Who'd kidnap me? Surely you'd choose someone easier to manoeuvre.'

'Don't be silly. I'm sure there are plenty of people who would kidnap you.'

'Thanks, Mum. That means a lot.'

'You're welcome,' Bertie replied with a flash of teasing. 'Are your bags with you? They haven't been stolen?'

'They haven't been stolen.'

'Are you hungry?'

'Is that a joke? You've packed me enough food to feed a small army. A large army, in fact, travelling several continents overland.'

Bertie chortled. 'Well, you'll need your strength. Winifred's a firecracker. A loose one that's gone awry and is now sparking randomly.'

Rowan's laughter met her mum's. 'What have you put me up to?'

'Despite appearances, Winnie can teach you a thing or two, you know. There's nothing like learning practical skills from a madwoman. The best kind of schooling. Plus, you might have fun!' Bertie instilled her voice with cheerfulness. 'I spent several summers in Coedyllaeth when I was young and I always loved it. Winnie and I running around like wild things. And anyway, she always wanted a child but she never had one and she's been asking for years to have you stay. It's time. Plus, you didn't send her a thank-you card last Yuletide, so this is your chance to make it up to her.'

'I'm being exiled to the middle of nowhere in Wales because I didn't send a thank-you card?'

'Not that you're dramatic.'

'Mum, this summer is critical socially. How am I going to compete when I go back to school if I've spent the entire time on a hill?'

'Winnie doesn't live on a hill. She lives at the bottom of one, and anyway, you don't need to compete. You're perfect already.'

'You're my mum, you have to say that. It doesn't make it true.'

'I only speak the truth and the occasional necessary green lie, but that isn't one of them.'

'I'm going to die alone.'

'Not that you're dramatic . . .'

'I learnt from the best.'

'You know there *are* boys in Wales. If I recall from my sixteenth year, some rather handsome ones. Dark and rugged—'

'MUM! Too much information. Anyway, there aren't any at Aunt Winifred's.'

'Actually, she has a boyfriend.'

'What?' Rowan exploded. 'You didn't tell me that! Aunt Winifred has a boyfriend. She officially has more of a life than me. I may as well adopt her cats now.'

'Maybe she can teach you a few tricks.'

'I am *not* taking love advice from Aunt Winifred. Last time I saw her she was wearing a hat with half a garden on it.'

'She does like her hats – I'm coming Gardenia!' Bertie yelled. Rowan could hear a ruckus in the background. 'Your sisters are driving me mad – no, don't touch that! – take care now, my socially destitute child. I hope you survive Winifred.'

'I might try and get myself kidnapped before I arrive.'

Bertie cackled. 'Farewell then, if we don't meet again – I said don't touch that!'

'Bye, Mum.'

'But also, call me when you get to Winifred's. And maybe just before bed to say goodnight – GERANIUM, LOOK WHAT YOU'VE DONE—'

The phone cut off.

Rowan dropped it on the table and dropped back against the seat. She missed her mum already. She missed home. She even missed her sisters. Well, maybe not yet, but she would. She looked at her reflection in the window and, for a brief moment, didn't recognize herself amid the rough hills and wind-shaken trees. Then she nodded at herself like a soldier might nod at a comrade before going into battle. She was Rowan Greenfinch. She did not give up. Like her mum often said, you can always make jelly from a hawthorn berry. She'd make the best of the summer, whatever was in store for her. She'd use her time away from the business of her family life to do the things she'd always meant to do, like exercise and school reading. She'd go on morning hikes, maybe she'd start a blog about living off-grid, or take up photography, or learn to paraglide. She'd return to school transformed – fitter and tanned and enlightened. *Could you tan in Wales?* And who knew, there *could* be a summer fling waiting for her in Coedyllaeth. Maybe she'd find someone to kiss.

She settled back into the unfolding drama of the landscape and let her imagination run wild through the fields ahead. Perhaps she'd go on a walk . . . lose her way and be rescued from a bog by a local farmer's son . . . dark and rugged . . . a dreamy smile . . . arms strong enough to push an ox up a hill . . . *did farmers do that?*

Rowan's thoughts were lost amid a tumble of hay bales when the train clacked slowly into a station. The sign came into focus: *Coedyllaeth.*

She jumped up. 'My stop! That's my stop! STOP THE TRAIN!' she shouted to the empty carriage. 'Shiiiiiit.' She gathered her belongings together and yanked her bag from the overhead rack, hurtling down the carriage and only falling twice before she got to the train door. She pressed the open button repeatedly before realizing it was the wrong door. She veered to the other side and burst out onto the platform, dropping Bertie's bag of treats – cakes spilling everywhere. She gathered them together and pulled herself up straight. She was used to dramatic exits.

No one else disembarked. The train pulled away with a sigh. She'd left from London Paddington but this station was no more than two platforms – one for each direction of travel – and a quaint stone building brightened with hanging baskets of summer flowers. It was empty save for a woman sitting on a single bench. Rowan knew from the hat it was Aunt Winifred.

Aunt Winifred stood up and faced her squarely. Rowan walked over, waving enthusiastically. 'Hi, Aunt Winifred!'

Aunt Winifred did not smile. 'Hello, Sorbus.' Sorbus was Rowan's actual name – the Latin name for the Rowan tree – though she did her best to hide it from the world. 'You're late.'

'Always.' Rowan grinned. 'But to be fair, I think it was more the train's fault than mine this time.'

Winifred blinked. 'A Hedge Witch never blames her tools.'

Rowan wasn't sure how to respond. They assessed each other with equal uneasy suspicion. Aunt Winifred looked nothing like any of the members of Rowan's family. She wasn't technically an aunt, but a cousin of her mother – first or second, Rowan couldn't remember, her mum had about a million. Winifred was tall, sinewy, and sturdy, made up of jutting angles that didn't seem to quite fit together. She was wearing a floor-length, sleeveless lilac dress as if to soften her staunch figure but it had the opposite effect. A large hunk of shrubbery was attached to her straw hat, all leaves and sprigs, a few stray flowers flapping over the brim. Beneath, her light hair was cut short and her eyes were wide and owlish, one of them sharp as shears and the other occasionally veering off in a different direction as if it was seeing something the rest of the world wasn't privy to. Her mouth was wide and her jaw stiff, but Rowan knew she wasn't as formidable as she looked.

Winifred moved forwards and gave her a rigid hug. 'You've grown.'

'Upwards or outwards?' Rowan cracked a smile. 'To be fair, the last time you saw me I was ten.'

'What are you now?'

'Fifteen.'

'Hmmm,' said Winifred, with the disinterest of someone who couldn't tell apart a ten-year-old from a fifteen-year-old. 'Either way, you look big enough to work a hedge. Strong of arm.'

Rowan peered down at her arms. 'I guess I'll take that as a compliment . . .'

'You should. Nothing wrong with being robust.'

Rowan crossed her arms around herself. She'd been called many things in her life – chubby, tubby, bubbly, curvy, plain old fat . . . but never robust. At least it was unique. She reimagined her gravestone:

Rowan Greenfinch: Robust and Strong of Arm. Still Died Alone.

'Right! Greetings over! To the car!' Winifred chivvied, setting off at a pace. 'We have a drive ahead of us.'

Rowan hurried after her. 'I thought the town was only twenty minutes away?'

'It is.'

The car looked as if it was held together with tape – a small, disconcertingly battered and bruised 2CV. Rowan put her bags in the boot and noticed that the exhaust was, in fact, secured on with wire. The front passenger seat was covered in debris – a watering can, plant pots, a basket of flower cuttings.

'Oh,' said Winifred, as if accommodating another passenger had never occurred to her. 'They can go in the back.'

Rowan squeezed herself into the front seat, pulling the belt around her. Several minutes later she was clinging to the seat, the belt, and herself, while Winifred hurtled with vigour down the small lanes of rural Wales, veering dangerously close to the hedges. She seemed to have only one eye on the road, the other roaming out of the window. Rowan closed her own eyes as they took a bend at speed.

Winifred turned to look at her. 'So, you intend to be a Wort Cunning?' The Wort Cunnings were the witch grove that Rowan's entire family and most of their extended friends belonged to, including Winifred. They worked with the magic of plants, though everyone had different specialities.

Rowan clutched the seat, wishing Winifred would look back at the road. 'Er – yes. Yes. Definitely.'

'Good. The Wort Cunnings are the most respectable grove out there and it's in your genes.'

'It is,' Rowan agreed. *If my genes survive this car journey.*

'Any idea what type of plant magic?'

'I think, probably, living plant spells like my mum.'

'Hmph.' Winifred pursed her lips. 'Your mother always was so strait-laced.'

No one in the history of Rowan's life had ever called her mum strait-laced.

'Well, it's the magic I've been doing my whole life,' said Rowan. 'And—MOTHER HOLLE!'

Winifred screeched the car to a halt in the middle of the lane. Rowan looked at her, but Winifred didn't seem to register what had just happened, continuing the conversation. 'It's certainly an interesting branch of magic but you ought to consider other options, like hedgecraft. A much more rigorous form of plant magic. Multidisciplined. Multi-layered.' With that, she extracted a pair of shears from the glovebox and exited the car. She stood in the road, staring at the hedge. Rowan waited, not sure what to do. She was used to strange relations but she'd never been so entirely reliant on one. Winifred continued to eye the hedge for several more minutes and then with a quick clip of the shears cut away a branch. She returned to the car and laid the cutting in the basket.

'Hedgecraft is not easy, mind you.' They pulled away errat-ically, almost crashing into the hedge on the other side. 'It takes a lifetime of dedication for those who have it in them. It's demanding – both physically and mentally.'

'Right.' Rowan gripped the seat again. 'Guess I better make sure to do my morning push-ups then.'

Winifred nodded firmly. 'Indeed. Now roll down your window. You can start learning right away. Take in the hedges! Britain is a land of proud hedges – sturdy, grand, wild, multi-farious – and Wales – Wales has the finest of them all. Breathe them in!' she commanded, her voice soaring in pitch.

Rowan slowly wound down her window, wondering if it was too late to find an excuse to return to London. She could throw herself out of the window and into said hedge, break various bones and *have* to be sent back.

'There is nothing more glorious in this world or any other than a July hedgerow!' Winifred pealed.

Rowan breathed the air in, blasted by the scents of summer – new grass, leaves simmering in the sun, heady puffs of pollen and bursts of flower. The hedge could barely contain them, colours of every hue spilling forth; long-necked cow parsley swatting at the window. Rowan put a hand out and let them run through her fingertips, beginning to relax, when Winifred slammed the brakes on again.

It took them almost an hour to get to Coedyllaeth, after

trailing a tractor for several miles, slowing for a pheasant to cross the road, and Winifred stopping to get out every few minutes to scour the hedges. Rowan occasionally checked her phone in the hope of signal, but there was none, not even a trace. *So help me Goddess.*

They crossed over an old stone bridge spanning a wide, slow-moving river, and the town appeared suddenly, trees giving way to houses. They drove into the centre which appeared to be little more than a single, higgledy-piggledy high street, the buildings clustered tightly together as if they'd crept closer over the years to keep warm from the cold winds blowing down from the hills around them. The centre had the same old-world charm as the station – stone pavements, neat shops, a war memorial ringleted with flowers; flags strung across the road flapped restlessly against the stillness of the quiet street.

Rowan peered through the window. 'Is this all of it?'

'Where would the rest be?' Winifred responded. 'It's got everything you could need. A greengrocer's, butcher's, hardware store, bookshop, and a library, which is more than most towns in Britain these days. There's no Costa What's It or Starbucket, if that's what you're after.'

'Starbucks?'

'Nor that! And if you insist on such frivolities, the bookshop café does a perfectly good cup of tea for a fifth of the price. Now.' Winifred stopped the car abruptly, Rowan jolting against her seat belt again. 'I've got to get a few bits. Wait here.'

She exited the car and disappeared into the Co-op. Rowan looked around, not entirely sure if Winifred had parked the car or simply left it sitting in the middle of the road. It seemed to allow just enough space for the other cars to move in single file around them. Rowan waved sheepishly at a passing driver and sank lower into her seat. She checked her phone again – still no signal. She was alone. Adrift. She scanned the high street searching for anything or anyone of interest, but considering it was a Saturday afternoon, there was hardly anyone around: a few elderly people movingly gingerly between shops; a mum with a pram; a man with a thick beard, an eye patch, and a leather waistcoat outside the pub, drinking a pint. He narrowed his unpatched eye at her and looked away. A black cat ran across the road.

The hill at the head of the town rose abruptly, gathering clouds and their shadows around it. The whole place had a strange atmosphere that Rowan couldn't quite put her finger on – as if it had been set adrift too, lost amid an ocean of hills, waiting for something to happen—

Rowan spotted an outbreak of action ahead and leant forwards.

Several people had gathered outside a building grander than the others along the street. It had a proud stone face, stately pillars, and high windows. The people were looking up and pointing at a large clock that hung out from its centre. They appeared to be in deep discussion. Something wasn't right with the clock. Rowan squinted, trying to work out what it was. The face was a blur . . . it appeared to have no numbers . . .

The door opened with a screech and Winifred clonked back into the front seat. 'All done,' she said. 'To home!'

'What's going on over there?' Rowan asked, pointing at the people.

'Oh. That.' Winifred coughed tightly. 'The town hall clock melted.' She started the car.

Rowan turned to her. 'Er – what? What do you mean, it melted? Clocks don't melt.'

'No,' Winifred agreed, pulling out without looking. 'Not that I know of.'

They drove past the town hall and Rowan took a closer look at the clock. She could see it now. The numbers had poured down its face and gathered in a senseless heap at the bottom. Time warped and distorted. 'But – but – how did it melt?'

'The cowans have concluded it was a freak natural phenomenon. The glass front of the clock magnified the sun's rays and liquefied the face.'

'Is that what you think happened?'

'The clock has been there for over two hundred years, so I think it's highly unlikely, but if they're happy to accept that explanation then that is all that matters.'

'Was it magic? You think it was magic? Did someone do it? Do you know who did it? Are there other witches here? Do you—'

Winifred put a hand up, straight as a clock hand. 'Do you always ask so many questions?'

'Yes. I've only just started—'

'Well, you can finish them there. My mind is busy enough without busying itself with the town gossip. There are more hedges ahead.'

Winifred's jaw clamped shut and Rowan could see she would get nowhere. At least it gave her something to think about for the rest of the journey. She'd accepted that she'd be living inside Winifred's mad world for the summer – but this wasn't in Winifred's world. It was the real world, albeit a small, strange town miles from anywhere. But even in the middle of nowhere . . . clocks didn't just melt.

Winifred lived outside of Coedyllaeth, down a narrow, single-track lane that seemed to go on forever. When they eventually pulled up at the end of the driveway, Rowan still couldn't see a house – only a large hedge. It towered over them, dense as brick, bulging with foliage and clustered with flower heads, like tiny blinking eyes watching them arrive. They nodded sagaciously in the wind.

'Do you actually live *in* a hedge, Aunt Winifred?'

'Yes,' Winifred replied, stepping out of the car.

Rowan had been joking, but she wasn't entirely sure if Aunt Winifred was.

Winifred rapped on the car window. 'Are you coming?'

Rowan followed her along the hedge until it was broken by an arch over a small path. Rowan was relieved to see a little cottage roosting within.

'I live *inside* a hedge,' said Winifred, turning down the path. 'I value privacy.'

'Well, you've certainly got it,' Rowan replied, passing beneath the heavy shadow of the hedge.

The cottage within felt dwarfed by it. A squat, stubborn little building, bobbled with white stone, seeded with tiny windows, and sprouting a chimney from its slate roof. Winifred had to take off her hat and bend down to get through the front door.

'Are you sure we can both fit in this house?' said Rowan, with a laugh, eyeing up the narrow hall.

'My house is a perfectly adequate size.'

'I didn't mean – I just meant – your house is lovely – very cute. Not cute. Er – charming. I'm thoroughly charmed. I love what you've done with the decor – so many different patterns – is that paisley?'

Winifred gave her a look, tucking her chin in. 'Has anyone ever told you that sometimes saying less can achieve a great deal more?'

'Many times, actually. But my mouth never seems to learn.'

'Hmph. Come on, I'll show you where everything is. I want you to feel at home here.'

The tour did not take long. Downstairs was no more than a kitchen, living room, dining room, and study. Upstairs – bedrooms and a bathroom. The rooms were small and snug as a matchbox, cluttered with old antiques and faded seventies furnishings. The beamed ceilings hung low and the hedge overshadowed the windows, and yet, despite the cramped feeling, there was a cosiness too, in the pots and pans and paintings dotting the walls, in the way the old oak floors creaked beneath your step, in the smell of smoke from the wood burner in the living room. Rowan wanted to drop into the room's large sofa which was sunken with use and piled high with patchwork cushions and Welsh wool blankets. There was no TV but the shelves were stacked with books, a few of them sprouting greenery from their pages. A little cuckoo clock on the wall began to chime. 'Cuc-koo! Cuc-koo! Cuc-koo!' Rowan startled as two wooden birds flew out from behind a leafy wooden hedge, flapping round and round the room. One of them landed in the shrubbery of Winnie's hat. 'Shoo.' She brushed it away, taking her hat off. She nodded to the clock. 'A gift from a Hedge Witch friend of mine. Strange woman. Now, to the kitchen, I have some extra wild garlic on the boil and it tends to get rather unruly if it's not stirred.'

The kitchen sat at the centre of everything. It was as busy as Rowan's home kitchen but there were no stews stirring themselves on the hob, no cakes baking in the oven, no cookies waiting on the side – this wasn't a space for nibbling and nattering, but a hive of industry. Plants hung from the ceiling beams, the shelves were stacked with jars and bottles, the surfaces were covered with a variety of equipment – baskets of cuttings, large bubbling canisters, bottles wired up to funnels and sieves and spiralling tubes that dripped and fizzed into a collection of containers. It was like the inside of a clock, everything turning and ticking to order. It smelled of cut herbs, the sweet tang of things fermenting, the clean sting of vinegar.

Rowan looked around. 'No cats?'

'Cats!' Winifred repeated, affronted. 'Why would I have cats?'

'I just thought – don't worry—'

'I've no time for the demands of pets. I have a hedge to take care of. You'll see,' she added with a touch of foreboding.

With that, the back door swung open and an anorak holding a bucket tumbled through it. The man beneath met them with an eager smile that ran ahead of him. He held up the bucket like a prize fish. 'A bountiful morning!' he proclaimed, pulling back his hood. He strode over to Winifred and gave her a kiss on the cheek. 'You wouldn't believe the size of my mushrooms!' He dropped the bucket down on the kitchen table, the loamy smell of fungus percolating into the air.

'You never fail to deliver, Llew!' Winifred cheered, the concentrated frown of her face dissolving as she looked at him. 'Sorbus, this is Llewelyn, my partner. Llewelyn, this is Sorbus.'

Llewelyn glanced up from the bucket with an animated smile. 'Hi!' He was younger than Aunt Winifred – at least ten years. He had a thin face, brown hair that rippled like a pine cone, and big soil-brown eyes that weren't really looking at her at all – they were lost elsewhere, still in the forest, flitting with eager curiosity, the quick calculation of a sparrow as he surveyed his morning's haul. He moved like a sparrow too – dipping muddy hands into the bucket, pulling out mushrooms, holding them up to the light, inspecting his treasures. He held a large one out towards Rowan, so close she could barely focus on it. 'Have you ever seen such a beauty?'

'Well – I, er—' Rowan stood back, trying to match his enthusiasm. 'It's impressive. I like its . . . colour.' She wasn't sure how to compliment a mushroom.

'Exactly!' he exclaimed, pleased with her response. 'It's a saffron milkcap. Delicious pickled. Look at these!' He pulled out several spongy mushrooms. 'They're called hen of the woods. Have you ever eaten one?'

'I don't think so—'

'Then you haven't lived!'

Rowan was well aware that she hadn't lived, but she didn't think eating mushrooms was the solution.

'I'll make pie tomorrow!' Winifred pronounced, taking them off him.

'You *really* haven't lived until you've tried one of Winnie's pies.' Llewelyn snorted a laugh. 'Ah! Where are you going?' He caught a mushroom that was rising up out of the bucket into the air.

Rowan's eyes widened. 'It's flying!'

'Floating,' Llewelyn corrected. 'The cloud cap mushroom. Not easy to find, but very special – eat them and you'll find yourself floating too. Now, if you like that, you'll like this one—'

He took another mushroom from the bucket – it was small and neatly formed, with a delicate silver body. Where he touched it his fingers disappeared. 'They call them fairy bonnets. You can find them in little rings in the forest and if you stand inside them you'll disappear. They'd be useful for hiding from bears! If we had bears in Wales!' He heehawed another laugh, already moving on to his next assessment.

'Cool,' said Rowan. She picked the mushroom up from the table and watched her fingers turn invisible where they touched it. 'I didn't realize there were magical mushrooms out there—'

'Of course there are!' he responded, as if it were the most obvious thing in the world. 'Not so many in London but, out here, in the wild Welsh woods, there are magical mushrooms galore – of course only witches can spot the magic ones, but they're abundant! Mushrooms beyond your wildest fantasies or funguses, as I like to say. That's a pun.'

Winifred released a high, startled laugh. 'Very good! Very good!'

'Right, I must go and write down my findings. I like to keep track.' He and Winifred kissed, long enough for Rowan to feel uncomfortable. 'Love you, Winnie Pooh.'

'Love you, Llew.'

He picked up the bucket and headed towards the door, stopping and turning back to Rowan, his eyes taking her in for the first time. 'A stump puffball!' he declared.

'What?' she said.

'When I meet someone new, I like to think of what mushroom they remind me of. You're a stump puffball!' He smiled widely as if he had just bestowed her with a great honour. Rowan tried to work out if he was teasing her but he looked at her earnestly.

'Er – thanks,' she said bleakly. *Stump puffball* did not sound like the kind of mushroom she wanted to look like.

'You are very welcome.' He nodded and left.

Winifred turned to her. 'Isn't he marvellous? He must like you, that's one of his favourite varieties.'

'He's – er – he's unique,' said Rowan. 'A real fun guy. Get it?'

Winifred frowned. 'I don't get it.'

'Fun guy. Fungi . . . it's a pun, as well . . .'

Winifred shook her head. 'It doesn't quite work, sorry. Right, now that you're all settled in, Sorbus, I must go and see to the hedge. Best not to disturb me. I need to concentrate.'

'Actually, Aunt Winifred, if you could call me Rowan. I prefer it.'

'Rowan.' She nodded. 'Well, if we're getting down to familiar terms already then you may call me Winnie. Not in public.'

Rowan nodded. 'Winnie, it is.'

Winnie smiled at her briefly.

'Oh, and could I get the WiFi password?'

'What's a why thigh?'

'The WiFi?'

'Feefo?'

'Doesn't matter.'

'There's plenty of food in the kitchen if you're hungry.' With that, Winnie was gone.

Rowan was left in the kitchen, like a spare part, not sure what to do with herself. She waited a while to see if Llewelyn or Winnie might come back, but they were both busy with their respective tasks – Rowan caught glimpses of Winnie beyond the window, wrestling with the hedge. Growing hungry, Rowan searched the fridge but it was full of bottles and jars labelled as various herbal decoctions. Winnie had bought eggs, sardines, and dental floss from the Co-op. Not exactly a feast. Rowan managed to forage some baked beans from the back of a cupboard and made herself beans and a fried egg. She ate dinner amid the busy apparatus of the kitchen and then returned to her allotted room.

It was a little space, half lost in roof, its ceiling sloped so that she had to bend down as she moved around. Its window, at least, sat higher than the hedge. Rowan looked out at the view – there was so much of it, field blurring into field, steely statues of sheep, undulating hills and forests, distant mountains sinking slowly into the inky mists of evening. More sky than the clouds knew what to do with. Rowan unpacked her belongings into the cupboard and sat on the bed, munching her way through her mum's treats, not used to quiet evenings. There was no TV. No Internet. She checked her phone a few more times in case signal had miraculously appeared. It had not. How was she meant to keep up with the summer gossip now? Obsess over everybody else's lives? She was severed – severed from everything: normal life, normal people, any hope of a normal summer.

She went to the bathroom at the end of the hallway and got herself ready for bed. She paused on her way back – Winnie and Llewelyn were having a conversation in the kitchen. She felt she ought to go and say goodnight, but, as she began down the stairs, she heard the word clock and stopped.

Winnie's voice oscillated. 'A melting clock is one tick too far.'

Llewelyn sighed. 'I don't know what's going on, but you shouldn't let it get to you. There's nothing we can do.'

'First, the ivy growing all over the war memorial overnight. Ivy doesn't grow that fast! Now the town clock melting . . . thank the Green Goddess the cowans have decided on an explanation but we both know it's not some solar phenomenon. Magic is involved. I'm sure of it.'

'All the more reason for us to stay out of it.'

'I intend to,' Winnie agreed. 'But I still don't want it to be happening. This town is my home. It's home to many witches and we've built a careful, if not friendly, balance here. But these events – they're upsetting it . . . the cowans' feathers are getting ruffled . . .'

'It might be the last of it,' said Llewelyn, soothingly.

'Oh, I hope so, Llew. I don't like surprises.'

'I know, Winnie Pooh. I know. Now, come here.'

They went silent and Rowan presumed they were hugging. She hoped they were hugging. She crept back up the stairs to her room, her mind buzzing with their conversation. If she couldn't access school gossip, town gossip would have to suffice – especially if magic was involved. Ravenous ivy and melting clocks . . . she tried to make sense of it, but the only thing that seemed to link the events was their . . . strangeness.

Her phone went off. She answered.

'Rowan, are you there?'

'Mum, how are you calling me? I've got no signal.'

'You think that would stop me.'

'True.'

'Have you been kidnapped yet?'

'Yes. By Winifred. Save me.'

'Surely it's not that bad?'

'I've been compared to a mushroom.'

Bertie snorted. 'Send out an SOS.'

'I would but I'm imprisoned by a hedge.'

'Well, you'll have to stay put then. Are you well fed at least?'

'Yes,' said Rowan. She didn't want her mum worrying. Her mum was capable of vast amounts of worry.

'OK, well get some rest now. Say goodnight to your father.'

'Rowan.' Her dad's voice came on the line. 'Are you having fun?'

'Yes, Dad.'

'Is Mum badgering you?'

'Of course.'

'Better you than me—'

Rowan could hear the phone being yanked off him. 'All right, enough of that,' said Bertie. 'Get to bed now, my little mushroom.'

'Mum!'

'Night, love.'

'Night, Mum.'

Rowan hung up and lay down, but she couldn't sleep. She found the moon outside her window. Half a moon. Turned away, like the sail of a boat, drifting off into the darkness. Leaving her behind like the rest of the world. She breathed out and could hear the motion of her breath. The house creaked. Rain began to fleck against her window. It was so quiet here. Back in London, she lived on a peaceful residential street, but even so – there was always noise. The drone of planes, the rumble of traffic, the startle of sirens, and people moving about – walking down the street, shutting doors, calling in pets – but here – here there was . . . nothing. Only the wind whistling through the bones of the house, as if it were lost.

Rowan had never felt so alone.

A GARDEN MADE
OF MOONLIGHT

The days passed slowly. Rowan counted them off like sheep – like the many bleating sheep that woke her every single morning. When she looked in the mirror she was becoming increasingly concerned by how closely her hair had begun to resemble their wild, woolly coats. She'd stopped bothering to brush it or wear anything nice – there was nowhere to go, nobody to meet. Nothing to do. Well, that wasn't quite true. There was plenty to do. Winnie kept her busy. It just wasn't anything she *wanted* to do.

Rowan sighed at the mound of dragon nettles beside her and freed another branch from the tangle. At least Winnie had taught her a charm to stop them stinging her fingers. They were the feistiest nettles Rowan had ever worked with, a special breed of Winnie's. Apparently, their tincture burnt like wildfire to drink but could cure a hundred ailments, while in their powdered form they could lend ferocity to spells of protection. Rowan put the branch on the kitchen table and began to pick the leaves away from it carefully. *Just the leaves*, Winnie had directed. *I don't want to find any stems and branches muddling my maceration!*

Rowan groaned – mostly for dramatic effect – feeling like Cinderella confined to the kitchen, lost among the canisters and crockpots, the drips and the drops, the bubbling of hedgerow wine and the gurgle of herbs boiling on the hob. No matter how much she did there was always more to do – plants to chop, bundles to tie, infusions to prepare, tinctures to filter, herbs to blend, blends to powder . . . and she hadn't even been allowed near the hedge yet.

You're not ready, Winnie said enigmatically whenever Rowan asked, wandering eye searching her out.

Rowan wondered if she would ever be deemed ready. In Winnie's defence, there'd been some . . . incidents already. Rowan had accidentally added mallow leaf to the chickweed tisane, rendering the whole batch useless; she'd burnt two days' of dog rose petal pickings to a crisp when drying them out, and she'd fallen off the chair while hanging herbs and cut her arm on glass. Winnie had put a plantain poultice on it that had healed the cut immediately, but Rowan hadn't even marvelled at the magic. She was used to making a mess of things but she'd never felt so hopeless. She wasn't accustomed to this kind of magic. Her mum's way of working with plants was different. There was a lot to learn of course, but it all unfolded gently, it was guided by intuition, you had to feel your way through. Winifred's was less forgiving. There were timelines and techniques and *specific* measurements. It felt all too much like chemistry, which happened to be Rowan's least favourite subject at school. Rowan didn't work in exacts. She liked to go into the garden, plant something, add a little spell, admire the flowers, lie in the long grasses and fall asleep watching the wind make patterns of the clouds above. *Away with the fey*, as her mum often said.

Well, she'd run out of daydreams to occupy herself. There were only so many ways you could imagine yourself running into the local farmer's son. There *was* no local farmer's son.

Rowan suspected there were no young men within a hundred-mile radius. She yanked another branch from the pile, being slightly less careful this time with her leaf picking. So much for experiencing the world. So much for becoming the woman she was meant to become. The only thing she was turning into here was a bloody stump puffball mushroom.

Outside, it was drizzling. Rowan swore it had rained every day since her arrival, as if the sky was caught in a protracted sigh it couldn't quite get out of. She spotted Winnie in the distance. She wasn't working on the hedge but standing still as a tree trunk and staring at it. Rowan had come to learn this was what Winnie called hedge trancing. She often did it for hours. Apparently there were all kinds of things you could do with a hedge beyond pruning, planting, and picking: *hedge trancing, hedge weaving, hedge dancing, hedge flying* . . .

Rowan didn't understand what most of these activities were, only that if you spent the majority of your time with a hedge – like Winnie – it would eventually turn you bonkers – like Winnie. Still, Winnie seemed content with her life. Her hedgerow products were highly sought after – she sold them to witches all over the country – and when she wasn't with her hedge she was caught up with Llewelyn, making stews and pies and occasionally odd puddings out of his mushrooms. They were always fawning over each other, *Winnie Pooh this, Winnie Pooh that* . . . Rowan had once walked in on them making out on the sofa, like teenagers. It had been horrifying. Horrifying to witness and horrifying that they were getting far more action than she was. She crunched on a biscuit despondently, losing concentration as she chopped the leaves and weighed them into batches. She was halfway through adding the batches to the bottles of vinegar when the contents of one bottle erupted into flame.

'FIRE!' Rowan shouted, jumping up. 'Maiden, mother, and fiery crone! FIRE! FIRE!' She realized that screaming fire wasn't going to stop the fire. 'SHIIIIIIT!' She ran to the tap and filled a glass of water and threw it over the burning bottle but it did nothing to dampen the flames. *Dragon nettle! Magical flames! They're magical flames!*

'By – er – the Green-Fingered Goddess, I command you to stop! Out flame, out! QUIT BURNING!' She directed her panicked magic at the vinegar but the fire had other ideas, leaping to the next bottle along. Rowan went back to shouting fire and ran out of the back door.

Winnie was in the kitchen in seconds. She gave the fire one hard look – the kind of look that could shrivel a mountain to a pebble. Abruptly, the fire abated. A ring of melted glass sank slowly into the table.

'Thank Mother Holle!' Rowan put a hand on her heart.

Winnie inspected one of the unburnt bottles. 'There is far too much in here, Rowan. It's no wonder it caught alight. My dragon nettle is incredibly virulent if not handled with care. The whole batch is ruined.'

Rowan looked up in apology. 'Oh, shit. Sorry, Winnie.'

'Don't swear, Rowan.'

'Sorry.'

'Stop saying sorry. It's not going to get us anywhere.' Winnie sighed like a dragon after breathing fire. 'You have to learn to focus. You have great potential but it's scattered all over the place.'

'I'll try.' Rowan pulled an upbeat smile. 'I promise. I'll focus the hell out of the next batch.'

'No more batches today,' Winnie replied wearily.

'I'm free?'

'You're free. For now.'

Rowan sat at the table, not sure what to do with herself. She'd already explored the house and garden several times over and, while she was bored, she was not quite bored enough to consider doing school work.

'You know, you could go for a walk,' Winnie suggested. 'There's a great expanse to be discovered beyond the hedge.'

'I'm not really a walker . . .'

'Do you not have legs?'

'I have legs. They're just unwilling.'

Winnie shook her head, exasperated. 'Well, I'm going to town if you wish to come.'

'Town?' Rowan jumped up. 'Now, that I'm in for.'

'I'm meeting an acquaintance.'

'Ooo, interesting. What kind of acquaintance?'

'Another plant witch.'

'A Wort Cunning?'

'No. A Moon Sower.'

'A Moon Sower,' Rowan repeated with wonder. 'I've heard of them, but never met one. Don't they sow plants by the moon? Special lunar varieties?'

'Yes. Wafty magic if you ask me, none of the rigour of hedgecraft, but they have some useful plants which I occasionally work with.'

'I'd love to meet one.'

'Well, you can, but I'm leaving immediately.'

Rowan put her hands up, backing out of the door. 'Give me two minutes – five minutes. Actually I need to brush my hair – ten minutes? It's going to need some work.'

Winnie looked at her watch. 'You have eight minutes and forty two seconds.'

Rowan, knowing not to argue with Winnie's nonsensical logic, ran from the room.

They parked haphazardly outside a small café towards the bottom of town: *Beti's Vintage Tearooms* the sign declared in curly, vintage script: *The best cream teas in Wales!*

'It's discreet,' Winnie explained.

The old pink awning was faded and the windows were

draped with dusty-looking lace. The door tinkled as they entered and Rowan was met with a headache of frill and flower – the wallpaper, the lampshades, the tablecloths – everything a clash of floral patterns. The tables were laid ready – teapots plump with woolly tea cosies and what Rowan presumed was meant to be a charming mismatch of teacups. Winifred marched a direct line through the flounce, heading towards the only occupied table where a woman and a girl were sitting.

Rowan's mouth dropped. She hadn't spotted anyone in Coedyllaeth under the age of forty, except a few children, but this girl was young, about her age.

The woman stood up. She was smartly dressed in a white shirt with bold silver jewellery. She had thick black hair and a warm smile, which crumpled the skin around her eyes like soft linen. 'Winifred, so nice to see you!' She squeezed Winnie on the arm. 'And who is this?' The woman turned her smile on Rowan.

Winnie spoke formally. 'This is Rowan. A daughter of my cousin. She's staying with me for the summer. Rowan, this is Ms Singhal.'

'Hi, Ms Singhal.' Rowan beamed. 'Lovely to meet you.'

'Do sit.' Ms Singhal sat back down and Rowan and Winnie took the two seats on the other side. 'Winifred, you should have said Rowan was staying with you! She looks about the same age as Laila.'

'Oh, yes.' Winnie looked between them. 'I guess so.'

Laila waved. 'Hi, Winifred. Good to meet you, Rowan.' She had black hair, swinging in a long plait down her back, thick as a rope. Her eyes were the blue-green colour of an ocean from above, distant and dreamy. They didn't look Rowan up and down with the critical reflex of most of the girls in Rowan's school, but instead met her eyes, her smile stretching from ear to ear. Rowan liked her instantly. She was about to reply when a woman ruffled over. She was as frilly as the café, decked in a floral apron with a puff of permed pink-grey hair. With her presence the flowers on the walls and surfaces – even the napkins – began to grow and bloom, over and over, making Rowan feel even more dizzy.

'More tea, dears?' the woman asked but didn't wait for an answer, picking up the pot. 'Earl Grey for you!' She poured tea into Laila's cup then swirled the pot. 'And green tea for you!' She poured a second helping into Ms Singhal's cup, the liquid coming out light green this time. 'More cream on those scones?' Again, the woman didn't wait for an answer, lifting a scoop from her apron and whipping it through the air. A thick wodge of clotted cream appeared inside it, which she dispensed on Laila's scone and then did the same for Ms Singhal. 'My cream is always cold and my jam is always warm!'

Rowan looked out at the street, at the people passing by.

'Don't worry, dear. Nobody can see through my lace curtains! Now, what can I get you both?' she asked in her thick accent, smiling perkily at Rowan and Winnie. 'A cream tea? Slice of cake? Welsh cake and butter? Or how about a milkshake? I can do any flavour you can dream of with as many cherries on top as you can eat!'

'Any flavour?' said Rowan, considering the possibilities.

'Except bodily fluids. I won't do them. It's just unpleasant.'

'A black tea, please, Beti,' said Winifred, sternly.

Beti looked somewhere between disappointed and disapproving. 'Are you sure I can't tempt you with a—'

'No cherries. I'm simply here to talk with Ms Singhal.'

Beti's lips pursed. 'As always, you don't know what you're missing, Winifred.' She swivelled to Rowan. 'What would you—'

'Actually, I think Rowan and I are going to head out,' said Laila. She looked at Winifred. 'Could I give Rowan a quick tour of the town?'

'What a good idea.' Ms Singhal smiled.

Winnie nodded her assent to Rowan. 'You have half an hour. We need to get back – the dandelion vinegars need filtering.'

'Yes, Sergeant.' Rowan saluted.

Laila stood up. Her outfit was whimsical and unusual for Coedyllaeth – a ruffled prairie dress with Dr. Martens boots and bright neon earrings. She slipped her arm through Rowan's and pulled her towards the door.

They emerged into the light. 'Oh, thank the Goddess,' said Rowan. 'That place was weird.'

Laila laughed. 'Welcome to Coedyllaeth.'

'I can't believe you're a real-life young person. You are real, right? Not just a figment of my socially deprived imagination?'

'You're funny.'

'Well, I think so.' Rowan grinned. 'But it seems to be lost on most people. So, what's in store on this tour?'

Laila looked up and down the near-empty high street apathetically. 'I wouldn't get excited. As you can see, there's not much going on . . .'

They began ambling up the street. 'I've noticed. So – er – do any boys exist in these parts?'

'Some.'

'Hold the wand.' Rowan stopped. 'Really?'

'Yeah. I hang out with two.'

'Two! That's one each!'

Laila chuckled. 'They're just old friends. I have a boyfriend actually, he's older, but he's gone backpacking for the summer. Finding himself.' She rolled her eyes.

'I see.' Rowan nodded, as if she understood the frustrations of boyfriends. 'Sorry, by the way, if I'm coming across as desperate and/or crazy – both of which might be true.'

'That's OK, this place will do that to you. Where are you from?'

'London.'

It was Laila's turn to look in awe now. 'Well, that explains it. You're not used to a slow-moving place like here. Goddess, I'd love to live in London. You're so lucky.'

'Have you been?'

'Yeah, but you know, just as a tourist. It was amazing. I saw three exhibitions at the V&A. I went shopping every single day. Have you visited the top floor of Liberty's?'

Rowan shook her head. Her family weren't exactly shopping people. If it didn't sell garden crocs, her mum probably wasn't going there.

'What?' Laila exclaimed. 'You have to go. You can get a dress made there out of anything . . . twilight, midnight mist, spring blossom, the surface of a lake, the waves of an ocean, the graffiti of a city . . . not that I could afford any, but still . . .' Laila swung around a lamp post, exhilarated. 'I could have stayed there forever.'

Rowan laughed. 'It's stupid really – when you live in London, you never make the most of it. I just hang out around the southeast where I live and go to school.'

'Do you know how many people go to my school here?' Laila looked at her flatly. 'Twenty-two. In total.'

'There might be some advantages to a smaller school.' Rowan thought of how many hundreds went to her own. 'Mine can be overwhelming.'

'I'd take overwhelming any day.' Laila stopped outside the newsagent's. 'Let's get some ice cream. The sun just came out. It doesn't happen that often. We must celebrate.'

'Well, twist my arm.'

The newsagent's was small and musty, made up of narrow aisles lined with heavily stacked shelves. Rowan could see cobwebs collecting between the higher-up products. The man behind the counter looked as if he'd been sitting there so long he'd started to melt into the seat. His eyes followed them, narrow and suspicious. They stopped at the ice cream freezer. Rowan picked one out, feeling uncomfortable. 'Does he always stare like that?' she whispered.

'Always,' Laila muttered. 'He thinks I'm going to steal something, which, of course, I never do.'

They took their ice creams to the counter and Laila put them down in front of him. His eyes trailed her movements, narrowing to matchstick slits. She smiled at him with childlike innocence. He turned to the ancient-looking cash register and hammered in the amounts. A pack of cigarettes gently floated off the shelf and hovered behind him. As if he sensed something, he twitched a glance over his left shoulder, but the cigarettes moved to his right. Rowan gulped at the act of magic, terrified they were going to be caught. Laila handed over the money, maintaining her smile. As he took it and put it in the cash register, the packet zipped through the air into Laila's hand. She slipped it into her pocket. His head whipped back to them, eyes screwed tight with suspicion.

'Thanks, Mr Pritchard,' Laila chimed. 'Have a lovely day.'

He growled something inaudible.

They burst back out onto the street. Rowan looked at Laila with disbelief. 'You – you – stole them!'

Laila unwrapped her ice cream. 'He shouldn't sell cigarettes. They kill.'

'But—'

'Didn't you ever want to steal something?'

'Never really occurred to me,' said Rowan, following Laila down the high street.

'You know you're a witch? It makes it pretty easy.'

'I guess, but isn't it, kind of . . . wrong?'

'Mum says there's no wrong or right, only context. We're Moon Sowers, we live by the light of the moon which is never one thing or another, it shifts and changes, finds its own balance. We call it moon-truth. Like, you don't have to steal from a nice hard-working person, you can steal from an overpriced megastore, or somewhere corrupt, or a store run by a man who's hated you ever since you moved into *his* town.'

'Mr Pritchard . . .'

Laila nodded, swinging a shop sign with her hand as they passed. 'I don't know if it's because we look different or if he senses we're *different*. Either way, he's always had a chip on his shoulder.'

'I'm sorry.'

She shrugged. 'Most people in this town are friendly. It feels like home, but there are always a few . . .'

'How long have you lived here?'

'My grandparents settled here when they were young, but Mum moved back here with me when I was eight. She was divorcing my dad and wanted the help. I think she missed the peace and quiet too.'

'It is peaceful.'

'You'd be surprised,' said Laila, raising her eyebrows, ice cream on her lips. 'There's more to this town than meets the eye.'

'Ooo, gossip,' said Rowan. 'Tell me all you know. As we've established – I'm desperate.'

'Well. You see her.' They were passing the local bookshop – Laila pointed at a woman working behind the desk. 'She's having an affair with the mayor. He puts on this big show of being a family man, but we all know they're doing it in the back rows of the shop.'

Rowan spluttered ice cream out of her mouth.

Laila laughed delightedly at her reaction. 'And see that woman over there . . .' She gestured her head towards an elderly lady crossing the street. 'She went to jail for drug smuggling.'

'Really?' Rowan replied, shocked. 'She looks so sweet.'

'Don't be fooled. That's before I even get started on the *witches* in this town.'

'Are there lots here?'

'Big time.' Laila nodded dramatically. 'A remote village surrounded by mystical woodland, with plenty of space and privacy – it attracts the most eccentric of our kind. You see that house.' She pointed to the top end of the high street.

Rowan spotted a black cat running across the road again and followed its path to one of the small, tightly packed townhouses. There were several other cats outside it and a couple curled up on the window ledges.

'The house is full of them,' said Laila. 'She's a Familiar Witch, works with her cats to cast. Supposedly every year she has a party where she invites other familiars from all over the country and they have a huge orgy, animals and all.'

'Ewww.' Rowan laughed. 'That can't be true.'

'Can't it? The local funeral director is a witch too. Divination. He can predict the exact day you're going to die and will draw up the gravestone in advance if you pay extra.'

'Dark.'

They stopped under the town clock. Rowan looked up at it, the numbers as melted as the ice cream in her hand. 'What about this?'

'Ah,' said Laila, with slow significance. 'You've heard about the strange events then?'

Rowan nodded.

Laila's expression turned serious. 'Everyone knows everyone's business in this town, but these happenings – they're a mystery. Mum has no idea. It's what they're talking about now. My mum and your aunt. Not that Mum really cares about it all, but Winifred's been on at her, so she thought it was best to meet with her.'

'Do you have any idea what's going on?'

'Not yet, but I'm working on it.'

'Aunt Winnie was worried it might upset the balance here . . .'

'It could. Magic is meant to be hidden away, isn't it? These happenings are all too public . . .'

'Designed to attract attention,' said Rowan.

Laila nodded.

'Gah – I want to know more, but my thirty minutes of freedom is up.' Rowan glanced behind them. 'Winnie is dementedly punctual. I better get back.'

They started down the street towards the tearooms.

'Maybe Beti is behind the happenings?' Laila smiled slyly. 'Her husband died a few years back and I reckon she poisoned him with one of her cream teas.'

'An arsenic-flavoured milkshake?' Rowan joked, but Laila nodded with interest.

'Yes! She could be turning her attentions on the town next. Who knows what goes on behind those lace curtains . . .'

'What about him?' Rowan tipped her head subtly towards the bearded man with the eye patch sitting in his usual spot outside the pub. 'What's his story?'

'Oh, Emlyn. He's nice. A witch.'

'A witch?' Rowan hadn't expected that.

'A Word Witch. He writes and recites beautiful poetry that can reduce even the hardest of hearts to tears.'

'Huh—' said Rowan, looking again at the burly figure, lifting a pint to his lips. 'Didn't see that coming.'

'He comes to my mum often for her moon sage. It's excellent for inducing inspiration.'

Rowan turned to her. 'I can't believe I haven't asked you anything about being a Moon Sower yet. Do you have a moon garden?'

'The most beautiful moon garden you've ever seen.'

'Really? Goddess, I'd love to see that. I've heard of them, but never seen one.'

'It's a full moon in two days,' said Laila, enigmatically.

Rowan was about to ask her more when Winnie called

from outside the bookshop. She looked agitated. 'You're over a minute late, Rowan! The vinegars will be ruined!'

Rowan made a face at Laila. 'I better go.'

Laila's smile pulled wide. 'Go save the vinegars.'

'Goddess help the vinegars!'

As Rowan rode back in the car with Winnie, hedgerows flying past them, she could hardly believe her luck. She may have made a friend.

Rowan lay in bed looking up at the full moon beyond her window – silent and far-flung, the night below meeting it with restlessness. She'd begun to realize that it wasn't quiet here at all, the night sounds were just more subtle than the din of London, but the more you listened, the more you heard: water dripping from the branches, the cold bleats of sheep, the hollow ring of an owl, the squelching croak of a toad, a stream dancing with itself, the wind tunnelling through the hedge, whispering with the leaves . . .

A knock on glass.

Rowan opened her eyes. That wasn't one of the night sounds.

The knock came again, a sharp rap against a window. *My window?* She sat up to another knock. It was definitely her window – but she was upstairs, how could someone be knocking on it? She lifted herself out of bed and went over to it, opening the window wide. A shadow was below. Her eyes adjusted to the darkness and she could make out Laila, her smile lucid in the moonlight. She raised her hand and made a knocking motion in the air – the knock came again on Rowan's window. She laughed and Rowan's laughter tumbled down to meet it. 'Laila! What are you doing here?'

Laila pointed to the sky. 'Full moon. No better time to see a moon garden.'

'I can't!'

'Why not?'

'Wait there! I'm coming!' Rowan went back inside, hurrying to locate the clothes she'd thrown off before bed. She left the room with only one sock and her jumper on backwards, and crept down the stairs. She needed to tell Laila that she couldn't go, that it was the middle of the night and she didn't have permission. It sounded lame even as she said it in her own head. Laila had come all the way here, was offering her friendship, a moon garden, a once-in-a-lifetime adventure . . . and she was going to say no. She had to say no. *Don't I? I do. Do I?* Rowan had never sneaked out before. Sneaking out was something cool people did, people with places to go and lives to live. *I wouldn't even know how to sneak . . .* But she *was* sneaking. She could hear Winnie's entirely oblivious snoring as she passed her room. Llewelyn muttered something in his sleep that sounded like the name of a mushroom. Guilt tugged at her – surely Winnie with her regimens and anxieties wouldn't approve. What if she woke up and found Rowan gone? She'd have a heart attack. A very high-pitched one. But then, it would be worse to wake her up to ask permission when she was so deeply asleep . . .

Rowan tiptoed downstairs, surprised by her own deftness, until she bumped into the hall table. She paused and listened but nothing stirred above. She turned back down the hallway and jumped at the sudden sound of the cuckoo clock.

'Cuc-koo! Cuc-koo! Cuc-koo!'

One of the wooden birds flittered towards her.

'Shhhh!' Rowan flapped at it. 'Go on! Back in your clock!'

The bird zipped away and Rowan ran for the kitchen. She let herself out of the back door and leant against the wall, giggling with sudden hysterics in the fresh night air. Cuc-bloody-koo!

Once recovered, she darted around to the front of the house. The night was cool and composed, the moon holding everything in check, the hedge draped in its light, like a slumbering giant wearing pearls. Rowan passed through its watchful gateway, hoping not to disturb it too. Laila was waiting on the other side, wearing a crop jacket and petticoat skirt that looked entirely impractical for the bike she was mounted on. Her hair was threaded with a white ribbon. She smiled and Rowan laughed. 'I can't believe I've just sneaked out! I don't think I've ever done anything quietly in my life! This opens up a whole new world of possibility. I could be a spy. A sleuth. A double agent.'

Laila met her laughter. 'You're coming then?'

'Oh. Well, I don't know.' Rowan looked back to the house, feeling the guilt tug again.

'You've come this far.'

'That is true – I just – think maybe I should wait to speak to Winnie . . .'

'But it won't be as fun if you have permission.' Laila's smile flicked up at the edges with daring. 'And it's the full moon *tonight*.'

'You make several strong points, but . . . how do I get there? I think stealing Winnie's car might be pushing the limits of my cool and, to be honest, I'm not sure it's even roadworthy.'

'I brought you transport,' said Laila, gesturing behind her, where a second bike was poised upright, waiting to go. 'I had to use magic to get it to follow me. It wasn't easy.'

'I can't believe you brought me a bike,' said Rowan, taken aback that someone would go to so much effort to hang out with her. She could hardly say no now.

'It's not far, a ten-minute cycle . . .'

'All right!' Rowan shivered with excitement. 'Come bane or boon, let's go!'

'Woo!' Laila cheered.

Rowan picked up the bike. 'I have to warn you, though – I'm not good on a bike. It takes all the skills the Green Goddess didn't bless me with. Balance. Coordination. Thighs that don't chafe. If I end up in a bush, you're the one who's going to have to drag me out.'

'Deal.' Laila smirked, then took off with speed.

Rowan wrestled with the pedals and sped off after her, cycling furiously to catch up, remembering just how bad at it she was as she careered down the small lanes, weaving all over the road.

She was hot, sweaty, and dishevelled by the time they arrived. 'Do you think bikes were originally designed as torture devices?' she asked, untangling herself from it and leaning forward to catch her breath.

Laila stepped gracefully from hers, petticoat floating into place. 'Come on, the moon is waiting.'

'The moon didn't just cycle up a hill . . .' Rowan muttered, but she rushed after Laila, lured by the pull of the moon garden.

Laila's house was bigger than Winnie's hedge-hidden cottage. A stone-fronted country abode with symmetrical windows and white hydrangea garlanding its face. Cars sat motionless on the driveway. They crept between the house and the garages through a little pathway into the back garden. Laila opened the gate silently and Rowan's breath left her . . .

Her own garden back home was her favourite place in the world. It was beautiful in a way that was wild and rugged, enduring and deeply rooted, at one with the earth, but the garden before her was not of the earth. If it wasn't for the faint tracing of Welsh hills in the distance, Rowan could have believed they had entered another world entirely.

The full moon shone bright as a mirror above them, the garden below reflecting its light in a hundred soft and silken, glistening ways, moving to the unseen tides of the wind. The flowers glowed white in their dark beds of foliage, drifting and dancing like dissolving petticoats; the grasses rippled like threads of silver coming loose; a tall water fountain cascaded with luminous, glassy waters. White blossoms and moon moths dappled the air with pale flashes, delicate and impalpable as breath. The whole thing felt fragile, weightless as a dream – as if it might, at any moment, float away. Drift back to the sky it had come from.

Rowan rarely experienced the sensation of being lost for words, but they had evaporated too.

'It's cool, right?' said Laila, skipping further in.

'It's . . . it's – the most magical thing I've ever seen.'

'You know Chelsea Physic Garden in London has a moon garden? You should go.'

'Really?' Rowan followed her in, trying to take in every plant, every flower. She didn't know half of them and most looked too fragile to touch, as if they might dissolve against her fingers. 'The Moon Sowers work with moonlight, right?'

'We sow plants that have a magical affinity with the moon and we sow by the moon too. I'll show you.' She beckoned Rowan over to a small stone structure.

'A dial—' said Rowan, only it wasn't quite like any sun dial she had ever seen.

'A moon dial,' Laila explained. 'It has three parts – see.' She pointed to a circle in its middle, where the stone was glowing – *could stones glow?* 'The centre lights up with the phase of the moon, so tonight, it's full. The next section' – Laila pointed at the surrounding circle which was carved with symbols – 'shows the position of the moon in the heavens. And the final circle' – she gestured to the outer circle which was writ with numbers – 'shows the lunar time. Everything we do in this garden moves to the motions of this dial – it's an intricate dance between moon phase, moon position, and the lunar time.'

'Wow. Sounds complex.'

'It's not really. I'm sure your own Wort Cunning magic seems complex if you're not used to it. Once you know your plants, it all sort of falls into place.'

Rowan nodded. 'I get that. Let the plants lead the dance, as my Uncle Sorrel used to say. He actually did dance with his plants. Big fan of the cha-cha.'

Laila laughed and wandered over to the stone wall surrounding the garden where white roses climbed, so delicate they were almost translucent, veined with light. 'Our moon plants are linked with emotional magic. Like these roses.' She cupped one in her palm and held it up to the moon's light – it blossomed open – a few of the petals drifted away. 'They're highly sought after for love spells, they open the heart to new love. We sow them when the moon is in Cancer and pluck them when it's waxing, like a heart swelling. They smell like heaven on earth.'

Rowan leant forwards to breathe in their scent. 'Not on earth,' she replied. It was dizzying, her own heart seemed to grow and ache under its spell, full of love and with nowhere to put it.

Laila moved on, brushing a hand through some flowers that tinkled like silver bells beneath her touch. 'Our lily of the moon valley offers peace to the most troubled of souls. Our jasmine brings happiness and inner riches, even to walk beneath it' – Laila passed through a trellis laced with jasmine so light it looked like snow fall; moon fall – 'will lighten your heart. Our moon-wort will unfurl your intuition, while our moonflowers' – Laila pointed to what looked like white sunflowers bordering the far wall – 'can be used in lunar rituals. It's where the word lunatic comes from – apparently when people observed lunar rituals they thought witches had gone mad, but that's only because they didn't understand the magic of the moon.'

They moved through the garden, blossoms flying, the flowers opening up their gentle lullabies, their mercurial magic. Heady fragrances filled up Rowan's senses and something else, something otherworldly she couldn't quite capture – like the cool, ephemeral light of the moon, it remained just out of reach. The water fountain murmured its own song, moving in miniature waves across each layer of stone and silvering over the edge into the one beneath.

'It moves to the tides of the moon,' said Laila, running a hand through the radiant waters. She pulled a water lily towards them, gesturing to its petals. 'Their petals mirror the wax and wane of the moon, so tonight they're all open, but as the moon wanes, the petals will close, bit by bit, night by night, until they seal up completely during the dark moon.'

'Amazing,' Rowan breathed, reaching for one through the cold touch of the flowing waters.

'We pick them during the dark moon too, when they're closed up. They aid in meditation spells, helping the mind turn inwards.'

'I could do with that,' said Rowan. 'My mind has trouble staying inwards, it's always far too outwards.'

Laila chuckled and took out the packet of cigarettes she'd stolen earlier. Rowan tensed, but Laila began to unfold one of them. She took a pinch of tobacco from inside and sprinkled it into the waters of the fountain. 'An offering – to the Goddess of the Moon.' She pulled a wry smile at the look on Rowan's face. 'You didn't think I was going to smoke them?'

'I was worried I was going to seem uncool if I refused, that I'd have to pretend I have asthma or something.'

Laila tipped the rest of the tobacco in. 'You don't have to pretend to be anyone else around me. I'd rather you be who you are, witch warts and all.'

'Well, I can confirm, I don't have any warts. Yet. I'm sure one day I'll be a warty, batty old witch but I've got at least a few years yet.'

Laila laughed and turned back to the water. She pulled out a necklace from inside her blouse. A silver, circular pendant, round as the moon. She began to unscrew it. *A container . . .* Rowan realized. Laila dipped it into the waters, collecting them. 'Lunar water,' she elucidated. 'Useful to keep on you. Adds potency to any spell.'

'Cool . . .'

Rowan and Laila continued to wander around the garden, time itself seeming to melt away. Rowan was starting to forget the other world existed at all when Laila looked up to her house. 'We better leave it there. Mum might be up soon to do some moon-sowing. We're a nocturnal bunch.'

Rowan returned to her senses. 'Thirteen moons! I'd better get back before Winnie stirs. She likes us all up at the crack of dawn so I should probably get *some* sleep.'

Laila led her back towards the gate. 'You're glad you came?'

'Are you kidding? It was worth every minute – even the cycle.'

Laila laughed delightedly. 'We can always come again now that you're so good at sneaking.'

'It is my main skill these days.'

'I'll take you back.'

They made their way out, Rowan drinking in the garden one last time, hardly believing it. Even if the rest of her summer came to nothing, she'd witnessed the magic of a *moon garden*. No one else at school could say that.

Their bikes were waiting for them on the lawn. Rowan mounted hers and walked it down towards the edge of the front garden; she was waiting for Laila to join her when she saw a figure ahead. She clutched the handlebars, imagining Winnie striding through the night to find her . . . but as the moonlight fell over the figure, Rowan could see it wasn't her aunt. It was a boy. Not just any boy. The boy of her dreams. Every single one. Ever.

Forgetting she was on a bike, she went to move forwards. Her feet caught on the pedals and she tumbled to one side into a bush.

STONES THE LAND GREW

Aslyn Davies One . . .
   Aslyn Davies Two . . .
   Aslyn Davies Three . . .
Rowan said his name as she counted out the mushrooms, sorting them into different bowls.

Aslyn Davies Fifty-Five . . .
   Aslyn Davies Fifty-Six . . .
   Aslyn Davies Fifty-Seven . . .
It wasn't the most practical name for mushroom counting but she liked the way it sounded in her head, the way it stirred the butterflies in her stomach into a frenzy. She imagined them like the moon moths, glowing just for him. Her daydreams had new life.

Aslyn was one of the boys Laila hung out with. What he was doing coming to hang out with her in the middle of the night Rowan didn't know but, as Laila had quickly cycled Rowan back to Winnie's, she'd talked again about how they were only friends. Not that it really mattered. *It's not like he's going to take any interest in me.* Rowan thought of him materializing from the moonlight – dark, curly hair falling over deep eyes, a face cut finely as the stars above. *He was perfect and I'm . . . the girl who fell in the bush.*

Rowan groaned at the memory and picked out two mushrooms from the bowl.

> *Aslyn and Rowan sitting in a tree,*
> *K–I–S–S–I–N–G!*
> *First comes a kiss, then comes love,*
> *Then comes a spell and a pinprick of his blood!*

She brought the mushrooms together to kiss.

'What are you doing?' Winnie's voice startled her. Rowan
dropped the mushrooms back in the bowl, cheeks beetrooting.

'Nothing.'

Winnie narrowed her eyes. 'The mushrooms must be ready
for tonight.'

'Almost done.' Rowan smiled. Winnie and Llewelyn were
having a few friends over for a 'mushroom party', whatever
that entailed. Rowan was sure it would be weird. However, it
was convenient. She had plans of her own. *Secret plans.* Laila
had stopped by a few days ago under the guise of delivering
some plants. She'd told Rowan they were all meeting up tonight
and insisted she join them. The butterflies in Rowan's stomach
scattered and clenched back together, excited and nervous.

'I thought we could go outside today – to the hedge,' said
Winnie.

Rowan jumped up, clattering the bowl to the floor. 'You
think I'm ready?'

Winnie's eyes fell to the fallen mushrooms. 'Don't let me
regret my decision. But yes, I believe you are ready.'

Rowan began to pick them up eagerly. 'I am so ready. I
am hedge ready.'

'That is not a hedgecraft term, but come on,' Winnie chivvied. 'Wellies on! Gloves on! Bring honey! Bring hedgerow
wine! Shears!'

'Cheers!' Rowan hurrahed.

'No. Bring shears.'

'Oh. Yes.' Rowan followed her orders. They marched outside and, for once, it wasn't drizzling. The sky was a clear, blazing blue, as if Winnie had demanded that too. The silver scars of distant planes cut paths through it. They stood in front of the hedge – the largest and most abundant hedgerow Rowan had ever seen, dense with summer. Rowan had the strange feeling that it was staring right back at her and suddenly didn't feel quite so ready.

Am I being outstared by a hedge?

She looked at the plants within it and felt more sure. There was the soft down of hazel, the puzzle-edged leaves of hawthorn, a prickly ribbon of holly, pink shells of dog rose, wild strawberries ready for plucking—

She reached out to take one and pulled back with a cry. The hedge had thorned her.

'My hedge has vigilant bramble protections,' Winnie informed her.

'Bloody violent protections if you ask me!'

'Don't swear, Rowan.'

'It started it!'

'I thought you were hedge ready?'

Rowan acquiesced. 'I am. I am. Sorry, Winnie. Sorry – er, hedge.'

'Before reaching out and grabbing at things, you must first show your respect, make an offering.'

'The honey and the wine?' said Rowan.

Winnie nodded. 'Pour a little of each into the roots and let the hedge know that you wish to work with it. Clear and concise wording works best, I find.'

To most people the request would seem strange, but Rowan had grown up around people who talked to plants like old friends. Rowan opened up the honey and wine and poured a little of each into the feet of the hedge. 'By the Green-Fingered

Goddess and all that is fruitful, I ask that I can work with you today and learn, you know, important hedge stuff. If you could not thorn me again that would be ideal, but it's your decision, and I get that, I just think, if you give me a chance, we could get along and—'

Winnie suffered a sigh. 'I think that's enough. Now, try to touch the hedge again. Let's see if it accepts your request.'

Rowan reached out a tentative hand and this time was met with no resistance. She brushed her fingers through the thick foliage. 'I'm in, Winnie. I am in.'

Winnie put up a cautionary finger. 'For now. Maintain respect – hedges are sensitive creatures.'

The formidable hedge certainly didn't look sensitive. It moved in the wind like something alive, a big green lung, sucking and exhaling the air through every budding stem and bobbing flower head. Winnie's eyes were fastened to it, swaying along to its rhythm. 'A hedge can teach you everything you need to know about life.'

Rowan laughed and then stopped at the stern look on Winnie's face. 'Oh, you're serious.'

'Of course I'm serious. A hedge's gifts are myriad. It offers lessons of patience, of timekeeping, respect, resilience, balance, focus . . . Rowan, are you listening?!'

Rowan had become distracted by a butterfly. 'Sorry! Yes. I'm with you – continue.'

Winnie's jaw locked. 'I won't work with an empty head.'

'I promise it's only half empty.' Rowan attempted a winning smile.

'If you don't pay attention, you'll miss what's right under your nose and a Hedge Witch must see all, Rowan. Near and far.' Winnie turned to her with a look of great significance. 'For a hedge is an edge.'

Rowan held in her laugh this time. 'I guess, technically, it is an edge . . .'

'I am talking about something far beyond technicalities here!' Winnie responded, her voice rising with emotion. 'Where the sea meets the shore, where forest meets field, where mountain meets sky. Edges. Boundary lands. Betwixt-places where the fruits of life clash, fuse, create, and thrive. Edges are the most alive places on earth, the most fertile places within our minds.'

Rowan looked at the hedge, trying to comprehend Winnie's words. It stared back, its leaves fluttering indifferently.

Winnie took in a deep and mysterious breath, wandering eye as wide as the sky. 'Now, what lies beyond the hedge? That is the real question.'

'Erm, sheep?' Rowan suggested.

Winnie's eye latched on to her.

'Hills?'

'This is not a game of I Spy, Rowan.'

'I give up. What lies beyond the hedge?'

'Well, I'm not telling. You have to discover that for your-self. Now, let's begin.'

Several hours later, Rowan regretted her previous hedge-ready eagerness. She had presumed they might tidy a few stems, pick a handful of plants, but over the course of the afternoon, Winnie had her digging through the soil, cutting away branches, trimming tangles of foliage, de-snailing the leaves, carting away the detritus, lugging the watering can back and forth . . . Rowan pointed out that they could simply conjure small rain clouds to do the watering as she and her mum often did, but, apparently, Winnie didn't believe in using magic when it came to the toils of hedgecraft. *Hedgework should be hard work!*

As they laboured, Winnie plied her with information and instruction covering the ins and outs of hedge sowing, growing, and maintenance, as well as introducing her to its many plants. Rowan thought she knew most of them already, but of course, it was not to be that straightforward. Winnie grew her own varieties with her own selection of odd names . . .

'This is my brave arrowwort! See how it stands tall and sure!' – Rowan recognized the white-headed plant as yarrow – 'A poultice of the leaves will staunch a wound, while an oil infusion will clear bruises. A tisane of its flowers, if picked at midday on Midsummer's Day, will cleanse and sharpen the mind for ritual. A tincture of the stalks and roots will lend you courage when you need it most, but don't take too much or you'll lose all sense of sense and suddenly believe you can fly off buildings.'

Rowan tried to take mental notes but it was hard – the plants all had a unique array of properties that varied depending on which part of the plant was used, how it was picked and how it was processed and taken—

'My hush-hush slippers!' – foxgloves – 'As poisonous as they are purple but an infusion of the leaves will clean the nervous system and instil the heart with vigour. The powdered flowers if ingested will allow you to move about silent as the fey, while the dew, gathered at sunrise, can be placed upon the tongue in order to communicate with realms beyond our knowing. A plant has many layers, Rowan, and as a Hedge Witch we must know how to peel them back. Now, my golden trumpet' – a deep yellow honeysuckle – 'makes an excellent syrup to soothe the throat and clear the lungs. If dried and carried around in your purse, it'll bring you wealth, but don't get too greedy or it'll take back what it gave you. As an oil it can be burnt to bring sunshine and prosperity into the home, as well as increasing psychic powers to those so inclined . . .'

It went on, and on, until Rowan's mind was as muddled as her hands were muddy. How was she ever meant to learn it all? And that was before she started on how it connected up to the chemistry of the kitchen. She wondered what it must be like to live inside Winnie's head – like a well-oiled, industrious factory full of bizarre, moving parts that only made sense to themselves.

Llewleyn brought them out some cold squash on his way to town to pick up supplies for their party. 'How are you getting on?' he asked.

Rowan wiped her brow. 'I miss the kitchen.'

'Isn't she a tyrant?' he said, looking at Winnie with adoring eyes and giving her a kiss before heading off.

Rowan picked another snail out of the hedge, reminding herself she'd be free that evening – free and in the presence of *Aslyn Davies*. 'Goddess, I need a shower.'

Winnie looked over her shoulder. 'What?'

'I said – er – what a pretty flower . . .'

Winnie frowned as if the visual delights of flowers had never occurred to her. 'Its petals can be burnt for use in wish spells.'

Rowan sighed. 'Do you have all of your hedge knowledge written down anywhere?'

'No. Why would I?'

'For other people to learn . . .'

Winnie's frown deepened. 'I might be teaching you, Rowan, but hedgecraft is not a communal activity. It is one carried out alone. Just as hedges are edges, hedge workers are edge workers. We exist on the fringes of life. Outsiders.' Winnie said the word with staunch pride but Rowan shrank from it.

'But, do you not get lonely here? Llewelyn out in the woods all day and no neighbours for miles . . .'

'Of course not. I have my hedge.'

Rowan nodded, knowing from the set of Winnie's face there was little point in further discussion.

The sun was beginning its slow descent towards the hills when Llewelyn returned. The car door slammed shut. 'Winnie!' His chirpy voice sounded tense. 'Winnie!'

Winnie looked up, alert as a hare in a meadow. 'The wheelbarrow needs emptying,' she instructed Rowan. 'I'll be back in a minute.' She hurried off, garden skirt flapping.

Rowan waited a few moments and then crept around the side of the hedge closest to the car, straining to listen to their conversation.

'. . . another happening . . .' she heard Llewelyn say, his voice low and hushed.

Winnie took a sharp breath, as if to prepare herself. 'What?'

'All of the words on the signs have disappeared.'

'What?' Winnie's voice rose higher.

'All of the town signs – they're empty – blank – no words—'

'What?' Higher again.

'The words have gone missing.'

'I understand what you're saying, Llew, but it doesn't make any sense.'

'I know.'

'The cowans?'

'They're blaming it on vandalism, people are angry but the anger is proving a useful distraction, stopping them questioning it all too closely. It's not like the words have been painted over or chipped away – they've just gone . . .'

'Words don't just disappear. Every sign?'

'Every sign.'

'Holy hedges! What are we to do? I need to gather the witches of the town together. We need a serious discussion. Most of them don't want to deal with what's going on, but this can't continue! These happenings aren't going away – they're getting more strange. We have to understand who is behind it all and what it is they want . . .'

'Ow,' Rowan hissed. She'd been leaning against the hedge and it had pricked her. 'All right. All right. I get the point.' She crept back to where they had been working and hurried to empty the wheelbarrow before Winnie returned. Blank signs. Disappearing words. It was bizarre, nonsensical, disturbing . . . What was the point of it? Was it a joke? A game? Or . . . a warning?

Winnie came back around the hedge.

'Everything all right?' Rowan asked.

'Yes. Yes.' Winnie nodded briskly. 'All fine and well. Fine and well. Just discussing the plans for later. I think we better leave the hedgecraft here for today.'

'Oh darn,' said Rowan, trying to sound convincing.

She waited to see if Winnie might say anything more but she didn't. Instead, her eyes skittered over the hedge, distracted with worry.

'I'll go and clean the tools,' Rowan suggested gently.

'Yes,' Winnie replied vaguely. 'Yes. The tools. A Hedge Witch always cleans her tools . . .'

Rowan clunked them into the wheelbarrow and rolled it away, leaving Winnie looking deep into the hedge as if she might find the answers there.

Rowan turned on the tap. Her body was aching, her mind was exhausted, but anticipation had begun to flutter about in her stomach again. The night was drawing closer. Not only would she be seeing Aslyn, but now there was much to discuss with Laila about the happenings. And yet, as Rowan washed the tools, mud draining away, her mood sank – would it really be any different this time? Winnie's words came back to her, bitter as a foxglove. *Edge worker. Outsider.*

Rowan had always wanted to live right at the centre of life, the place where things happened, but those words were too close to the truth. She was already an outsider – she'd always been one. There were the people she sat with at school and hung out with at band practice but she wasn't sure she could call them *friends*. She had plenty of family to keep her occupied and life was never dull among the Wort Cunnings but even so – though she rarely admitted it to herself, she didn't always feel as if she fitted in there either. She was enthusiastic and willing and she loved nature, but she wasn't actually *that* talented at botanical magic. She could never imbue her plants with the same force of spell that her mother could. She was easily the weakest in her family and sometimes . . . sometimes it felt as if something was missing, as if the future that had been written for her was full of empty spaces, its own missing words.

She switched the tap off and tried to shake away her thoughts. She was being silly. She was just tired and hungry. She was a Wort Cunning through and through; she just hadn't found her calling within plant magic yet. That was all. She looked back at the hedge and wished it would stop giving her that look, like it knew something she didn't. Like it was peeling back her layers and not the other way around.

Rowan looked in the mirror. Her hair was bouncy, her outfit was flattering, she'd even managed to wash most of the snail off. She no longer looked like she'd been dragged through a hedge backwards, or in Winnie's world, backwards, forwards, and upside down. She pulled a few poses.

'Hi, Aslyn . . .'

'Hello, Aslyn, fancy seeing you here . . .'

She spun around, flicking her hair over her shoulder. 'What's up, dream boy?'

She was distracted by the noise of the gathering downstairs, the high peal of Winnie's laughter. Rowan had already said her goodnights, now she just had to find a way to creep out without them noticing. She'd almost confessed to Winnie several times, intending to ask permission, but she'd bitten back the words. If she asked, then Winnie could – probably *would* – say no. They were in the middle of nowhere; she wasn't going to let her go gallivanting about after dark. Rowan checked the time on her phone. Twenty minutes until she was due to meet Laila. Outside, the darkness was as clear as the day had been, the stars appearing one by one with bright promise. The night sounds had begun their orchestra too – bleats and barks and cries and caws, the hedge rustling with prickly secrets. Rowan waited, listening to it, until she realized it had gone strangely quiet downstairs.

She frowned and opened her door but was met with nothing but the usual creaks of the old cottage. Had they all gone outside? Rowan crept to the bottom of the stairway, then tiptoed down the hallway and edged along the wall to the living-room door, which was slightly ajar. *Spy. Sleuth. Double agent. We can do this.* She held her breath and peeked through the gap. She gasped loudly and slapped her hands over her mouth, pinning herself back against the wall again.

They were floating.

The gasp gave way to a laugh which she tried to contain. She took another glimpse to check she wasn't seeing things, but they were still floating. Winnie, Llewelyn, and a handful of equally eccentric-looking friends were hovering silently around the small room, bobbing against the ceiling beams, their eyes closed and distant inward smiles painted on their faces as if they were all listening to the same song, while Rowan couldn't hear the music. Winnie's tie-dye dress draped towards the floor, her large scarecrow form drifting as gracefully, as incongruously as a ballerina. The cuckoo clock birds darted about among them, as if just as surprised by the spectacle as Rowan.

Llewelyn's cloud cap mushrooms . . . it had to be! Rowan shook her head, still laughing to herself. At least it made it easy to escape. She suspected they were going to be out of the world for quite some time – if they ever entirely returned. She ran past the door and made her way quickly out of the house.

Laila was waiting for her at the bottom of the lane, the spare bike standing to attention behind her. 'What?' said Laila, sensing Rowan's disbelief.

'They're all high on mushrooms in there – and I meant that entirely literally.'

'What?'

'I find it better not to ask questions.'

Laila laughed but it wasn't quite able to sustain itself. She looked different, dressed plainly in jeans and T-shirt – and her smile, it wasn't quite as full, as if someone had turned the dimmer down on it. 'Shall we go?'

'Are you OK?'

'Yeah,' said Laila, shifting her bike around. 'Just want to get away. Let's go.' She took off with haste.

Rowan had no idea where they were going but she jumped on her bike. Fell off. Jumped on again and pedalled hard after Laila. Her legs were already sore from a day of hedgecraft and as they climbed towards town her muscles screamed in protest, but visions of Aslyn pulled her onwards. Laila slowed down as they passed the sign at the town entrance. It was blank.

'Did you hear what happened?' she said.

Rowan nodded and stepped off her bike. She walked over to the sign and ran her fingers along it. There was no trace of words having ever been there at all, as if someone had undone their stitching and dusted the threads to the wind. Rowan shivered. 'It's so strange. Signs without words . . .'

'A clock without time.'

'I just don't get the point.'

'Therein lies the mystery. Come on, we should go, the boys are waiting.'

'Boys! Let's go!' Rowan bellowed, making Laila laugh more fully this time. They set off, weaving through the dark high street, in and out of the pools of light from the street lamps, past the shuttered shops and vacant town hall clock. Laila took both her hands off the pedals and hooted. A light went on in one of the houses and they pedalled fast into the shadows to escape being seen.

At the top of the street Laila pointed up to the hill that overlooked the town. 'We just need to get up there.'

'A HILL?' Rowan cried. 'YOU DIDN'T SAY ANYTHING ABOUT A HILL! A hill is up! Up hurts. I don't think I have any up left in me.'

'You'll want to see what's at the top . . .'

Rowan wiped the sweat from her brow as they pushed their bikes up the last leg of the hill. It had been worse than it looked, steep and sharp. Laila parked her bike against a tree. 'We can leave them here.'

Rowan dropped hers on the ground. 'Is this' – she sucked in a deep breath – 'what you – guys – do for fun – around here? Midnight cycles up bloody mountains!'

She scrambled after Laila, and they broke through the upper line of trees onto the summit of the hill, which opened up into a wide, grassy plateau. The view knocked the breath from Rowan again. The valley unrolled before them, the town sleeping at the centre of it – a huddle of houses, a scattering of farms, moonlight making rivers of its streets, and beyond, fields and woods and lost, roaming mists – the hills gaining momentum, climbing up towards a slow explosion of stars above, the night's sky as deep as the valley below.

'As above, so below,' Rowan whispered, half dazed.

'Beautiful, right?'

Rowan turned from the view to follow Laila. Ahead, three monstrous figures crystallized from the darkness.

'Woah—' Rowan cried out and then stopped, realizing they weren't figures at all. They were stones. A circle of large, staggered rocks rising up from the ground, like a giant's fingers reaching up through the centre of the hill, grasping at the sky. Someone was reclining beneath them.

'Hey,' said Laila.

The person propped their head up. *Aslyn Davies.* Dark, but not particularly rugged. The moonlight painted a fine picture of him, flowing over his sanguine form, settling on high cheekbones, the curve of full lips. Entirely kissable lips. His hair gleamed black, falling in artful curls. He was wearing an unusual, bright patchwork jacket of many colours. He smiled up at them with smoky, sleepy eyes. 'Yo.'

Not exactly poetic but Rowan would take it. She smiled back, trying to find something to say and then tripped on an object beneath her feet. 'Gah—'

'Hey. Watch where you're going.' An irked voice rose up from below. It was another boy, sitting up against one of the rocks.

'Sorry. Sorry—' Rowan looked down at him. 'Didn't see you there. To be fair, it's pretty dark out here and I often struggle to see where I'm going in full daylight.' She laughed. The boy gave her a blank look and shuffled himself around to sit within the stone circle.

Laila intervened. 'Rowan, this is Aslyn, who you met before, and Gareth, who you just stood on.'

'Ignore him,' said Aslyn. 'We call him Gareth the Grump.'

Gareth grumbled.

'And we call him Aslyn the Asshole,' Laila retorted airily.

'Says Laila the Loon, who howls at the moon . . .' Aslyn gibed.

Laila laughed but the sound of it felt hollow.

Rowan tried to laugh along, feeling entirely like an outsider. 'Well, I'm just – Rowan.'

'Our honoured guest,' said Laila.

'I wasn't aware we were bringing guests along now,' Gareth muttered.

Rowan hovered awkwardly. She patted one of the stones. 'Big old stones, these!' she said, to fill the silence. 'Very . . .

upright. Good job I didn't walk into one of them, hey? Are they, like, a stone circle? I visited a few on family camping trips. Mum says they're magical places, always seemed like damp places to me. Haven't been to Stonehenge yet, but one day—'

'Wouldn't bother,' Aslyn interrupted. 'Overrun by cowans.'

'Of course.' Rowan nodded. 'That's what I thought. Who needs Stonehenge?'

'We do *need* Stonehenge,' said Gareth. 'All the stone circles across this country are connected. A network. They function as a whole.'

'Function,' Laila scoffed. 'You make them sound like machinery. They're not – they're magic.' She patted the ground beside her and Rowan sat down, glad to be on solid ground. The stones towered above them, black shadows condensed to rock. The night's sky seemed more alive against their stillness, the stars lighter against their density.

'They increase magic, right?' said Rowan. She knew that much.

Laila nodded. 'Exactly. They're like . . . charging points for magic. Supposedly they're arranged along the old Moonsong lines. They say that each year during the Seven's annual ritual they use the old lines, bringing magic to life across the country. I'm sure it's why this town attracts so many magical types. It sits right below them.'

Aslyn snorted, sitting himself up with effort. 'This town attracts crazy types.'

'Speak for yourself.'

'Hey, I don't live here.' He put his hands up defensively. 'Just dragged here every summer by my parents.'

Rowan glimpsed at him. 'Where are you from?'

'Hampshire, but my mum grew up here and she inherited the family house, so . . . yeah . . .. instead of going on an *actual* holiday, we come here. Every. Single. Year. I almost got out of it this time – tried to convince my parents to let me stay home. We argued for days and in the end they agreed that it could be my last.' He fist-pumped silently. 'Next year I'm staying put. I'm going to throw so many house parties . . .'

Laila nudged him. 'You know you'll miss us really.'

'I won't miss the wet and the wind and my dad insisting on taking me birdwatching. I swear I've been on like a hundred walks and I can't tell one from the other. Everything looks the same. It's a hill, it's a tree, it's a river, it's another bloody crested tit—'

'You don't get crested tits in this area,' said Gareth.

'You know what you do get? Sheep shit on your shoes.'

'You should wear more practical shoes.'

'But then I'd end up looking like you,' Aslyn retaliated. 'You're part anorak.'

Gareth huffed, digging his sensible walking boots into the mud.

'Be nice, Aslyn. Gareth and I have to live here all the time,' said Laila. 'We *are* the crazy locals. Anyway, Rowan's from London, which is far more interesting than any of our home-towns.'

Rowan shook her head. 'No. Not interesting. The London suburbs are like anywhere else, really.'

Aslyn raised his head. 'Where do you hail from?'

Rowan looked deep into his eyes and then remembered he'd ask her a question. 'Er – Forest Hill.'

He nodded as if he knew it. 'I've got some friends in Stoke Newington.'

Stoke Newington was nowhere near Forest Hill but Rowan nodded back. 'I've been there a few times.'

'Got friends there too?'

'Er – no. A cousin. He's big on ferns.'

'What?'

'He works with ferns. Magically, that is. My family are all Wort Cunnings. We pretty much have every plant species covered between us. It's why I'm here, to spend the summer with my Aunt Winifred, learning hedgecraft.'

'What?'

'Hedges. The magic of hedges. It's a thing . . . in some, weird circles . . .'

Aslyn nodded politely but his eyes wandered away. *Mental note: stop talking about hedges.*

'London's too crowded,' said Gareth.

Aslyn looked at him. 'Have you even been?'

'Yes. Once. On a school trip . . .'

Aslyn laughed loudly. 'A school trip! I don't think that counts.'

Laila's voice drifted over them. 'I'd love to live in London. You could spend every weekend dressing up and going to galleries, restaurants, clubs . . . you'd never run out of things to do . . .'

Rowan didn't want to point out that she'd never been to a club in her life and spent most evenings in her pyjamas watching reality TV reruns with her mum. 'What do you guys do around here for entertainment, then?' she said.

'You're looking at it.' Aslyn gestured languidly. 'We sit on a hill among a bunch of stones.'

'*Magical* stones,' Laila corrected. 'Show them some respect – they're older than Coedyllaeth. Older than the stars. Older than time itself.'

'Really?' said Rowan.

'Probably.'

'How did they get here?' Rowan asked. 'I don't know much about standing stones, they're not a common feature in London . . .'

'Technically, they're called Root Stones,' said Gareth.

'Oh—'

'Standing stones is a cowan term,' Laila added. 'Bless them. Cowans have driven themselves half mad trying to work out how they came to be. The number of theories on Stonehenge . . .'

'Not to be all cowan clueless here,' said Rowan, 'but how did they come to be? Did the Seven create them?'

Laila shook her head, eyes swallowing the stars. 'No. No. Before even the Seven. They were put here by magic itself.'

'The magic of the land,' said Gareth. 'It grew them.'

Rowan looked up at the stone above her absorbing the wonder of Gareth's words. *Grown by the land.* Like plants. Like trees. Branches of stone. *Who had planted their seeds? How deep did their roots go?* In the silence of the stones' mysteries she could feel something. It had been there all along but she hadn't noticed it – she realized it wasn't just one thing, but *everything.* Within the circle, everything felt heightened, more than itself, as if the stones were frets around which the strings of night were being slowly tightened. The cool air felt charged. Each blade of grass defined. Each drop of dew crystal-bright. The darkness above so deep, so finely tuned with stars that Rowan had a sudden sense of infinity and herself part of it. She had the feeling that if she released her breath the stones would turn it into a wind powerful enough to shake the trees around them. Everyone else was silent too, lost in the same dizzying magic.

Eventually Laila spoke, though her words came softly, as if not to disturb the wonder. 'Where do you think all the words went?'

Gareth grated a sigh. 'Not this again.'

Rowan realized what Laila was talking about – the town signs.

'We can't just ignore what's happening,' said Laila.

Gareth glanced at Rowan. 'We shouldn't talk about this now.'

'We can trust Rowan,' said Laila, flashing her a smile. 'She knows about it all.'

Rowan smiled back but Gareth mumbled something beneath his breath.

'It's like that lullaby of yours you were singing the other night,' said Aslyn.

'Oh yeah,' Laila recalled. 'My mum used to sing it to me before bed.' She began to recite it, her voice moving in gentle waves:

> *'Hush, hush, little darling,*
> *The moon rises bright,*
> *See how it shines,*
> *And casts out its light.*
> *Dancing on treetops,*
> *Alighting the flowers,*
> *Spilling o'er the earth,*
> *Raising its powers.*
> *But as the Crone knows,*
> *Spinning silver from flax,*
> *One day the dark moon,*
> *Will take it all back.*
> *Flowers from their shoots,*
> *The leaves from their trees,*
> *E'en the words of this song,*
> *Everything – disappeared!'*

Rowan shivered at the lullaby's strange forlornness.

'I can't believe your mum sang that to you. It's creepy as fuck,' said Aslyn.

'It's not.' Laila frowned. 'It's beautiful and weird like all the best things.'

'No, it's creepy,' Gareth agreed. He and Aslyn shared a smile.

'It doesn't explain what's happening though,' said Laila, ignoring them and looking out at the valley below, the town appearing so innocent in its sleepy guise.

'My aunt was really upset about the signs,' said Rowan. 'About what the cowans will think—'

'Cowans have no imagination,' Aslyn drawled dismissively. 'They always come up with some painfully dull explanation.'

'Do you guys have any idea who is behind it?' Rowan asked. She was used to knowing all the gossip, but she didn't know this town or any of the people in it. She was struggling to work out the strange dynamic between Laila, Aslyn, and Gareth before starting on anyone else.

'Don't start Laila on that . . .' said Gareth.

'Ignore him.' Laila rolled her eyes. 'Gareth lacks imagination too. I have loads of *ideas*. In a town full of this many witches, there are no shortage of suspects.'

Rowan leant in. 'Tell me all you know.'

Laila needed no encouragement. 'Well, it has to be a powerful witch. Older. Experienced. The magic is too advanced. My current theory is the Familiar Witch I told you about. Everybody knows she had a thing for the mayor. I bet she's found out he's having an affair with the bookshop owner and she's pissed – getting her own back on him by targeting the town. Her cats are everywhere, they could be spreading the strange magic – but then – it could be the Mutterer . . .'

Rowan looked bewildered.

'Old Mog Jenkins. He's a Mutterer Witch – mutters his spells beneath his breath. He lives on the edge of town, he's old and sour as blue cheese and hates everyone.'

'He's grumpier than Gareth,' Aslyn confirmed, earning himself a glare from Gareth.

'He's always complaining to the council about something or having spats with his neighbours. And last year, at the summer fete . . .' Laila took a dramatic pause. 'He won second prize in the marrow-growing contest.'

A laugh ruptured from Aslyn. 'He's cursing our town because his marrows were too small?'

'Not too small,' said Laila. 'They were the biggest and he *still* didn't win. That's why he's getting his own back. He believes they're prejudiced against him, against the likes of us.'

'That's so stupid,' Gareth grunted.

'Why? Revenge is a powerful motive.'

'So is attention seeking.'

'So are marrows,' Aslyn added.

Laila was not put off. Her voice sharpened and darkened, like the granite of the stones around them. 'Then, of course – there's Black Annis.'

'Who's Black Annis?' asked Rowan, trying to keep up.

Laila caught her in her gaze. 'The old witch of the wood. The wood that runs north of the town. There's a broken-down cottage there, abandoned and terrifying. So local legend goes, Black Annis lived there once, hundreds of years ago, and she vowed, one day, to return again to exact her revenge on the town.'

'Why would she want to do that?' Rowan breathed in.

'Because they killed her.'

'Who?'

'Everyone. The town. They suspected her of being a witch but before the authorities could organize a proper trial they dunked her in the lake to see if she'd sink or float.'

'And did she? Sink or float?'

Laila's smile fell away, leaving her face desolate. 'Some say she sank and disappeared and that no trace of her body was ever found. Others say she floated to the surface and carried on floating – flying away. Others say they let her go, but it was too late, that the Hunters were already on her tail and got her.' The wind wailed around them, unnerving the leaves.

'Every town has a Black Annis,' said Gareth, matter-of-factly. 'She's hearth legend. And there's no such thing as the Hunters.'

'You don't know that,' said Laila.

'I do. Everybody does. You're getting lost in your stories again, Laila.'

'I am not. I'm just open to all the possibilities. We don't know what's going on or what it means or if it'll get worse. What if this is just the beginning? What if the whole town descends into madness?'

'Then you could become mayor,' Aslyn replied. 'Laila the Loon, mayor of crazy town.'

'Shut up!' Laila kicked at him from where she was sitting. He grabbed her leg and she fell backwards onto the grass and began to laugh. It rose up through the stones, curling like smoke. She rested her head on the grass. 'Beautiful and weird . . .' she said, faintly, to herself.

Gareth sighed.

Rowan lay back too, beneath the vivid sky. 'I tell you what we don't have in London – stars like these.'

'This area has one of the lowest levels of light pollution in the UK,' said Gareth. 'People come from all over to star-gaze.'

'Imagine making a dress out of them.' Laila's voice glowed. 'A starlight dress. I bet you Liberty's has one. If it doesn't I'll make one myself.' She turned to Rowan. 'It's what I intend to do, my language: magical fashion.'

'I thought you were a Moon Sower,' said Rowan.

Laila shook her head sharply. 'My mum is a Moon Sower, not me. I don't want to sow by moonlight but to sew *with* moonlight.'

'That sounds amazing.'

'It will be. Got any inkling about your magical language?'

'Oh, I'm a Wort Cunning,' Rowan replied, without pause. 'I don't really know yet what *kind* of plant magic though. My mum works with living plants so maybe that. Anything but hedges, ideally.' She laughed. 'To be fair, some of the hedgerow plants are fascinating but—'

'I'm going to be a Dream Witch,' Aslyn declared. 'An Astral.'

Rowan spluttered a laugh. *Of course!* The boy of her dreams was going to be a Dream Witch.

Aslyn looked at her, affronted. 'What?'

'Oh – er, nothing. I just don't know much about the Astrals, they have a funny name, don't they?'

He looked at her as if she were an idiot. 'They cast spells in their dreams. It's, like, very powerful magic.'

'Cool,' said Rowan, making sure she sounded thoroughly impressed.

'I heard the most senior Astrals wear cloaks made of colours that don't exist in our world and their eyes turn to kaleido-scopes,' said Laila.

Aslyn nodded with authority.

'You just want to be a Dream Witch because you think it's easy as sleeping,' said Gareth. 'To become a real Astral takes decades of training. It's more than just casting dream spells, it's about mastering your own mind—'

'How do you know?' Aslyn sneered.

'Because I read stuff.'

'Well, maybe you should focus less on my language and start thinking about your own.'

'Do you feel drawn to any particular languages?' Rowan asked Gareth.

He shot her a look. 'No. Not bloody dream magic, that's for sure.'

'Something much more grounded for our Gareth, here,' said Aslyn. 'Maybe a Bog Witch.'

'I'd rather be a Bog Witch than a Dream Witch, thank you very much.'

'It's so exciting, isn't it?' said Laila, who seemed to have perked up since the start of the evening. She plucked a dande-lion seed head from the ground. 'Not knowing who we're going to be. What we're going to become. The possibilities . . .'

Rowan followed Laila's gaze upwards. She had never really thought about magic that way. She loved it, but it was like the ground beneath her feet: rich and fertile but reliable and rooted. A given. Not something so . . . floaty. The dandelion seed head rose out of Laila's hand. A small white orb, buoyed up by the wind, catching on unseen flourishes of air. Somewhere just beneath the stars, it dissolved into seed. 'Watch this,' Laila said.

Rowan gasped.

This time, every dandelion seed head in the grass around came free from its stem and rose into the air. Up and up. The heads beyond the stones dispersed – but within the stones they began to glow. Gently at first but then brighter. Brighter. A hundred tiny glowing moons rising up to meet the moon above.

'Woah.' Rowan exhaled. The trees stirred.

'You see?' said Laila. 'The stones make magic more powerful. They sing with it. They sing with the old Moonsongs.'

In that moment . . . Rowan could almost hear the music.

A SURPRISE OF BIRDS

After the stones, things felt different. The days began to fly like birds, measured out by passing clouds, bouts of sunshine, and bursts of drizzle. Whatever the weather, Rowan and Winnie spent their mornings out in the garden with the hedge, their afternoons in the kitchen: chopping, boiling, steeping, drawing the magic out of their spoils, and the evenings – the evenings were fuelled by the stars, Rowan had been meeting up with the trio every few nights . . .

She was due to meet them again at the weekend and could hardly wait.

'Pass the shears.' Winnie extended a hand and Rowan gave her a pair of shears and returned to her own hedge picking. Winnie hummed an unknown, sprightly tune as they worked. The hedge was rich with life this morning, butterflies and bees buzzing about and berries and fruit plumping along its stems. Rowan had to admit, she was starting to grow fond of the hedge. She liked how it never stayed still, how it was always changing, things dying back, new things growing, every day a different season in its world. It felt as if she was beginning to get to grips with hedgecraft too. Her muscles were knots, her arms scratched, her ankles stung, she still

caused several minor magical incidents a day and had to ask
questions constantly, but the dots of Winnie's methods were
slowly beginning to connect up – even if the dots were all
over the place and often contradictory.

Worryingly, Rowan had even caught herself staring at the
hedge yesterday . . .

Her mum had laughed on the phone. 'You'll be wearing a
hedge on your hat before you know it.'

'I will not! My hair is big enough without sustaining a
bush on top.'

Bertie hooted. 'Oh, I miss you, my girl.'

'I miss you too.'

'Have you spent any more time with that local girl, Laila?'

'Oh, a bit.' Rowan had lied. 'Now tell me all about home,
what's the latest?'

Rowan didn't know why she was lying to her mum. She
never lied to her mum. It wasn't like she was doing anything
bad with the others – they weren't drinking or vandalizing
or casting rogue spells – and she was normally home not long
after midnight, but even so, she was sure her mum and
Winnie would not be pleased if they ever found out. And
. . . she liked having a secret. It made her feel like an insider,
not an outsider, for once. She felt like if anyone else found
out it would all come crashing down, she'd wake up, as if
from a dream and remember she was only Rowan Greenfinch:
the odd, plump girl who no one wanted to hang out with.
Here, she had friends, even if she was still struggling to
understand the group.

Laila was hard to predict – sometimes she was the girl with
the sunshine smile that Rowan had first met that day in town,
but other times she was distracted and melancholy, lost in
her imaginings. There'd been a fresh incident – all of the
vegetables in the local allotment had exploded overnight.
Laila had decided it was clear evidence that the Mutterer was

responsible – that he was targeting the vegetables after the town had failed to appreciate his marrows, but the next time they met she already had several new suspects. Even Rowan, who prided herself on her proclivity for gossip, struggled to keep up with her theories.

Meanwhile, Gareth still didn't seem to like her no matter how much she talked to him, or *at* him. And Aslyn . . . Aslyn was still perfect and Rowan had no idea *how* to talk to him. She'd always had so much to say but around him anything she thought to say seemed somehow boring or inadequate. He never took much interest in any of her anecdotes about the Wort Cunnings or her jokes about what Winnie and she'd been up to that day with the hedge. *Of course not! He's cool and radical and wants to be a Dream Witch, not be told the different uses of chickweed root and how to find a stump puffball mushroom . . .*

She'd thought about revealing her crush to Laila but something held her back. There was a closeness between Laila and Aslyn she couldn't quite put her finger on, even though Laila always referred to them as friends and occasionally brought up her travelling boyfriend. But Rowan had never seen any pictures of this boyfriend and the details about him always seemed a little vague. Rowan was sure Laila was telling the truth, it was more likely that Aslyn simply wasn't interested. But then, the other night he'd sat down beside Rowan in the circle of stones and their knees had touched. Three times. He'd asked her what sort of music she liked. That was progress. He was taking an interest in her tastes, even if he then proceeded to talk for several minutes about how he was in a band back home while Rowan had stopped listening and imagined how good he'd look playing a guitar. Perhaps tonight he'd walk her home and their hands would accidentally touch and one thing would lead to another and—

'Rowan! Are you with me or has your head emptied itself again?' Winnie's words clipped like shears.

'Sorry, Winnie. Just away with the fey, as my mum likes to say.'

Winnie's eyebrows cinched together. 'The fey are never away anywhere, they are always exactly where they need to be.'

Rowan laughed but quickly realized Winnie wasn't joking. 'Er – OK. Do you want me to pick some elderberries next?'

'Yes, we'll need some for later, but be careful when taking berries from the hedgecrone,' Winnie directed, using her own name for the elder tree. 'You must ask nicely and don't take too many bunches from one tree. It can be a generous plant but it doesn't take kindly to being taken advantage of. It's very shrewd, incredibly wise. Its berries we can make into a syrup, or wine, or tincture – all excellent at chasing away winter colds, but if dried and eaten whole before casting they will sharpen the words of any spell, the stems make for astute wands, and the roots—'

'Can be boiled and taken as a tonic to access the wisdom of your ancestors.' Rowan finished her sentence.

Winnie nodded, a smile breaking through pursed lips. 'Very good. Very good. I'll make a Hedge Witch of you yet.'

Rowan didn't know whether to be pleased or concerned by Winnie's comment. 'I'm not sure I'll ever be able to learn it all though.'

'Learning is only part of hedgecraft. Seeing is more important.'

Rowan nodded. Nodding was the best response when Winnie said something that made little sense.

Winnie's eye began to wander, which was never a good sign. Her voice lost its abruptness, turning misty. 'A hedge has many levels, Rowan, many levels, and a Hedge Witch must live between them all.' Her head tilted to one side. Rowan tilted hers too, trying to see what Winnie was seeing. 'Below and above, within and beyond. To know not only what a plant can do, but what it can open up, for they are keys to other worlds. Do you see?'

'Kind of.'

'Wrong answer.' Winnie wandered down the hedge. She plucked a berry from a tree. It was bright orange. She held it towards Rowan, a bright flame in the morning light. 'You ought to know which tree this comes from.'

Rowan smiled, taking the berry. 'The Latin name is *sorbus*, but it's commonly known as the rowan tree, or mountain ash.'

'I call it lightning ash. It has the brightest berries in the bush. They are radiant and plucky and powerful.'

'Goddess knows why my mum named me after them, then.' Rowan grinned.

Winnie did not look amused. 'Rowan, are you aware how often you put yourself down?'

Rowan closed her mouth. No one had ever said that to her before.

'You ought to learn from your namesake. Do you know why this is one of the strongest plants in my hedgerow?'

Rowan shook her head.

'Because its berries open up one's inner power, which is the greatest power of them all. A place without limits. But first, you must *see*.'

Rowan looked at the hedge again, not sure what she was meant to be seeing. She could see the many plants she knew the names of. She could see a bee disappearing inside a flower. She could see the breeze moving through it all, bringing everything into a rush of life.

'What do you see?'

'Well, I—'

'Beyond the hedge—'

'Er—' A flock of birds flying above the hedge distracted Rowan. There was something wrong with them. 'Birds,' she said.

'Birds?'

'Birds . . .'

Winnie followed Rowan's gaze upwards. 'Birds,' she echoed, dumbfounded.

The birds weren't flying forwards – but backwards.

Rowan blinked, but she wasn't imagining it, the birds *were* flying backwards, wings flapping in the wrong direction, tails leading the way. They had been so focused on the hedge that she hadn't really looked at the sky that morning, but now she took it all in with creeping unease – it wasn't just one bird. It was all of them. A passing crow. A pair of pigeons. A startle of nearby sparrows. All of them . . . flying backwards.

'B – b – birds!' Winnie squealed. 'What's wrong with the birds?'

'It's proof!' said Laila, eyes exultant with excitement. 'I've been thinking it over since it happened and it has to be the Familiar Witch – if she can control cats, she can control birds.'

'For Goddess's sake, Laila, leave it alone,' Gareth snapped, even more ratty than usual.

But Laila continued, weaving a pathway through the stones. The town sat below them beneath its unassuming quilt of darkness. You would never have thought that a few days ago birds had been flying backwards through the sky. 'But then—' Laila stopped. 'Maybe I'm barking up the wrong tree.'

'Barking would be the word,' Gareth murmured.

'Didn't the old legends say that Black Annis could take on the form of a bird or a bat? That she could fly through the night and into people's dreams? Maybe it's her! Maybe she's the one who messed with the birds.'

'Or maybe it's the milkman! Or maybe it's ninety-eight-year-old Mrs Ogmore! Or maybe it's me!' Gareth spoke with rising exasperation. 'Or maybe . . . this whole thing is completely ridiculous.'

Aslyn snorted. He was leant against one of the stones in his usual multicoloured jacket. 'It was quite funny watching all the cowans outside, pointing up at the sky, trying to work out if they were seeing things or not.'

Rowan had not found Winnie's distress amusing. 'Winnie thinks it's gone too far now. I mean, how many natural phenomena can one town get away with?'

Aslyn released a laugh. 'It's hardly going to make the national news. Nobody cares about this place.'

Laila stood up. Tonight she had dressed up again, a floral minidress and waistcoat, her hair in two buns on the top of her head. 'We should go to the ruins!' she announced. 'We should see if they've been in use recently. If Black Annis is back.'

Gareth groaned. 'There's no such person as Black Annis.'

'We don't know that until we've been to the house! Come on – it's not far . . . twenty minutes' walk.'

'Can't be bothered,' said Aslyn. 'Can't we just hang here?'

'It'll be fun!' Laila ignored his protests. 'A haunted house at midnight. Come on.' She nudged him with her foot. 'Don't be boring, it's our last summer. Pretty, pretty, pretty, please. Pleeeeeeease. You know I won't give up.'

Aslyn groaned. 'You never give up.'

'I don't.'

'Fine. Whatever. We'll go to the stupid house.'

Laila cheered. 'Rowan, you're in, right?'

'Er, well—' Rowan did not think it sounded like a good idea, but Aslyn *was* going. 'Sign me up. I've been meaning to go for a walk, why not now? In the dark . . . through the woods . . . with a potential lunatic witch on the loose. I'm sure it's recommended in all the guidebooks.'

Laila chuckled. 'Come on then! Let's go. We should try and be there for midnight, it could be the height of Black Annis's powers.'

'The only thing this is the height of . . . is stupidity,' said Gareth, flatly.

Laila turned to him. 'You're not coming?'

'Obviously, I'm not coming. That house is structurally unsound.'

'Structurally unsound,' Aslyn repeated. 'You sound like a health and safety officer. Maybe you're just too chicken to go . . .'

'I'm not scared.'

'Chicken, chicken.' Aslyn began to cluck.

'Come on, Gareth, you know you want to really—' said Laila, trying a different tack.

'No, Laila. I'm tired of your persuasions. I'm going home. You should all do the same.' He gave Rowan a stern look.

Aslyn clucked louder.

Gareth put his hands up. 'It's up to you. But be warned, Aslyn. You're going to ruin your shoes.'

Aslyn stopped clucking and looked down at his white sneakers with concern.

They gathered themselves together and left Gareth on the hill among the stones. Rowan glanced back at him, wondering if she ought to have stayed. She wasn't sure she entirely trusted Laila's judgement.

They stumbled down the hill, away from the safety of town and towards the forest. It rushed to meet them at the bottom like a dark wave, branches rippling. Laila took a torch out of her bag. She turned it on. Its light was softer than a normal torch but powerfully illuminating, stripping the branches silver and setting the leaves aglow. 'A moon torch,' she explained.

It made the forest look as otherworldly as her garden but, even so, the shadows still gathered. Rowan swallowed a nervous gulp in her throat.

'So this, er, Black Annis character. Why did they suspect her of being a witch?'

'All the usual reasons,' said Laila. 'But I also heard that if you came up against her she would send her midnight imps to suck the life out of you. You'd wake the next morning unable to move, sapped of any joy.'

'Oh good.' Rowan nodded as Laila disappeared into the trees.

Rowan took a deep breath and followed. Within, the silence was sudden and oppressive. Nothing but the sound of leaves fidgeting, twigs snapping beneath their feet, a wind too hollow to be comforting. A far-off screech raised the hairs on Rowan's neck.

'What was that?' Laila clutched Aslyn.

'Probably just a fox,' he said, but his voice was dry, the edge of mocking long gone.

The forest tangled thicker around them until they shuffled together along a narrow path, even the moon torch struggling to penetrate the branches ahead.

'Are you sure we're going the right way?' Aslyn asked.

'I think so,' said Laila. 'I've been in the day, but it's harder to work out at night . . .'

'Maybe we should just go back—' he began to say, but Laila pointed ahead.

'There it is! There!'

The house was hard to spot. It looked as if it had crawled out of the forest floor, a muddy rubble of stone, half consumed by branches and ivy. They edged closer and Rowan could see the glass of the windows was shattered and jagged like the remains of teeth. There was still the vague form of a front door though the wood looked half rotted. A slur of graffiti shone neon along its front, the words: *SHE DEVIL*. Rowan tried to ignore how the prickle in her neck was now crawling all over her body like something alive.

'That's the house,' said Aslyn, his voice thin.

'Yes,' Laila whispered. 'We should go in. Investigate.'

Nobody moved.

'Aslyn . . .'

'To be fair,' said Aslyn, slowly. 'It does look a bit structurally unsound . . .'

'True,' Laila agreed. Maybe we should just leave it . . .'

Rowan looked at them. 'I thought we came all the way here to go in?'

'You know what . . .' Laila ran a foot through the leaves. 'It's probably not Black Annis. Too obvious. It's probably someone right under our noses—'

'I'm going in,' Rowan declared, surprised that the words had just come out of her. She thought of Winnie, how panicked she'd been watching the birds, how disturbed she was by the whole thing. If there was a chance they could discover something, she had to check . . .

'No, Rowan. Don't,' Laila cried. 'Let's go back.'

But Rowan took the moon torch off her. 'I'll be quick as a sleuth.' She broke away from them before she could change her mind. She directed the torch to the forest floor beneath her, watching her every step. This was not the time to stumble. It was also better than facing the house – the house that looked as if it had been torn from a storybook and then torn up again, broken into nightmarish pieces that no longer fitted together.

Rowan shuffled towards the front door – roving the light over it – seeing flashes of peeling paint and deep scratches in the wood. She reached out her hand and touched the handle. It was a shock of cold. Wet and slick.

'Gross.' Rowan recoiled. She focused on the handle and opened it with a burst of magic. Gingerly she pushed at the door, which seemed to push back, clogged with ivy and rubble. She kicked them away with her foot and stepped through.

Inside, the house was worse. Its innards broken and twisted, hinting at rooms that used to exist but were now near unrecognizable – the walls crumbled, the floorboards caving in, ivy drooping from the old beams above. It smelled of damp that had turned solid, sludge that had hardened like rust. Rowan inched forwards, shining the torch over the devastation. The light flashed over an old wooden chair missing a leg, the remains of a fire on the floor and some discarded beer cans. One was sprouting nettles. There were the beginnings of a staircase leading to nowhere. No signs of life. The house had not been touched for a long time.

A sound above ruptured the silence.

Rowan shrieked and dropped the torch. It went out and darkness rushed in to fill the horrors around her. She scrabbled about for the torch with desperate hands, the prickles in her body sharp as knives now, telling her to *get out, get out, get out!* Her hand found the torch and she grabbed it, switching it on and swinging it around the room, terrified at what she might find – but there was nothing there. The sound had come from above.

Rowan moved the torch slowly higher, not wanting to know what it might reveal. Higher, higher – up to the rafters, to the contorted remains of an old chimney . . .

A shadow came at her out of the darkness.

'GAHHHHH!' Rowan turned and ran. The thing, the creature, the monstrous form chased her. She could feel it around her head, flapping in her hair.

She flew out of the house, limbs flailing, scream erupting, and ran straight into a figure. Arms caught her. The arms of Aslyn Davies.

Rowan opened her eyes and looked up at him. He looked down at her. It was the most romantic moment of her life – except for the fact they were both about to die.

'Something – something – chased me,' Rowan stuttered.

There was a hoot above them. They stared up. The monster was sitting in the tree above them.

'It's a wood pigeon,' said Aslyn.

Rowan assessed the demonic form. 'Ah – yes. It is.'

Aslyn let her go. 'Are you OK?'

'Of course I'm not OK. I've just been viciously attacked by a wood pigeon.'

She managed to laugh and Aslyn joined in. She took several deep breaths as he steadied her. She glanced up and their eyes met. Her heart was thudding, but she wasn't sure anymore if it was because of what had just happened . . . or his sudden proximity. His face was so close a kiss was entirely feasible, wonderfully possible.

'Rowan,' he said.

'Yes . . .'

'You're standing on my shoe.'

'Oh.' She picked her foot up, seeing that she'd left a smear of sludge along his sneaker. 'Sorry.'

Laila appeared beside them. 'What happened? I heard screaming—'

'Rowan only just made it out alive,' said Aslyn, pointing up to the tree.

The wood pigeon hooted and they descended into laughter. The kind of desperate laughter that follows on the tails of fear. Once she'd recovered, Rowan straightened herself up and ran a hand through her hair, pulling out several twigs. 'I did get a good look inside though.'

'And?' Laila asked.

'Nobody has been in that house for a long, long time. I'm sure of it.'

They looked back at the house. Now Rowan had ventured inside, it didn't seem quite so terrifying – just some old, forgotten ruins in the woods. She realized how ridiculous their entire expedition had been. How had she been so caught up in Laila's theories?

'It could still be Black Annis,' said Laila, as they made their way back down the path. 'Just because she hasn't returned to the house doesn't mean she isn't out there somewhere . . .'

'Maybe she's rented a nice apartment in town,' Aslyn suggested drily.

Laila hit him. 'I'm keeping an open mind . . .'

'Maybe she really IS the wood pigeon.'

'Aslyn . . .'

'Maybe we should capture it and torture it until it tells us the truth.'

The conversation grew more and more ridiculous, until they spilled, with giddy relief, back out into the field. A figure loomed out at them from the darkness. This time they all screamed.

'Black Annis!' Laila cried.

'No. Just me.' Gareth put his hands up.

'Gareth!' Laila yelled. 'Goddess of the Moon, what are you doing out here? It's pitch black!'

'I know my way around,' said Gareth. 'I was coming to find you guys. I was concerned. That house really is unsafe . . .'

'We're fine,' said Laila.

'So, did you go? Did you complete your dumb mission?'

'We did. Rowan went into the house.'

Gareth looked at Rowan, surprised. 'You went in?'

'Well . . . just a quick peek.'

'And?'

'And it will forever haunt my dreams, but I didn't find anything.'

Gareth made a face at Laila. 'Surprise, surprise, no Black Annis. You shouldn't have let Rowan go in alone, that was completely stupid—'

'It's done now!' Laila cut him off. 'And we're going home.'

Rowan checked the time. 'Yeah, it's getting really late. I need to get back.'

'I'll take you guys,' said Gareth. 'I know a short cut. You coming, Aslyn?'

'I left my bag up at the stones, I'll make my own way back.'

'Why don't you just get it in the morning? Come with us now,' Gareth insisted.

'Who are you?' Aslyn sneered. 'My mum? I can get myself home.'

'We'll see you soon,' said Laila, interrupting their spat.

Aslyn began up the hill but then called out, 'Oi, Rowan!'

She turned around. He smiled at her and for a brief, hopeful moment she thought he might ask her to go with him instead. 'Look out for the wood pigeons!'

She laughed. 'You too!'

He snorted a laugh back, and made his way back up the hill, dissolving into moonlight.

FLYING A FLYING KITE

Music blared from the radio. Elderberries hovered in the air in uniform rows, bouncing along to the song like footloose soldiers. Rowan directed the berries into the open bottles on the table, while chopping up the meadowsweet she'd picked that morning. She spun herself to the cupboard, fetching the alcohol and pouring it in quick dashes into the open bottles. She conducted the remaining berries into a large vat and began mashing them ready for the elderberry syrup. She left the masher going of its own accord while she went to check the dandelion, yarrow, and broom she'd left steeping a few days ago. She breathed in their pungent aromas and returned to the bottles, shutting the tops and giving each one a shake while shaking herself along to the music. She was in flow, twirling around the kitchen, her mind in several places – and pots – at once, her senses absorbed by the demands of hedgecraft, daydreams of Aslyn weaving through it all.

She remembered their moment in the woods with a loop the loop of her heart. The way he'd held her. The way he'd looked into her eyes. The way he'd called her at the end of the night to tell her to watch out for wood pigeons. It was their joke. They had a joke. She imagined him bringing up the anecdote at their future heart-knotting ceremony:

We first realized we were in love after fearing for our lives at the hands of a vicious wood pigeon . . .

She danced the final bottle around the kitchen but stopped when she saw Winnie in the doorway.

'No need to cease dancing on my account,' said Winnie, bustling through. 'I've been known to get jiggy myself while preparing a tincture or two—' Her face fell. 'What's that smell?'

'The gooseberry jam!' Rowan cried, rushing over to the pot on the hob, but it was too late, it had already begun to burn.

'Damn Mother Holle, I forgot to reduce the heat—'

'Don't swear, Rowan.'

'Sorry, Winnie.' Rowan looked at the spoiled jam. 'The scatterbrain strikes again. I thought I was getting better at this but I've made a mess of things as always—'

'Don't be silly. A mess is just a lesson in the making. Even the most experienced Hedge Witches make mistakes.'

'You don't.'

'Well, that's only because I've made so many over the years, I've run out of them.' Winnie took the pan off the heat and carried it to the sink. 'Hedgecraft is not learnt overnight. It takes a lifetime of dedication for those who have it in them.'

Rowan had started to enjoy hedgecraft, but the thought of a lifetime overwhelmed her. She couldn't imagine it, but then it was hard to imagine dedicating her entire life to any one branch of plant magic.

'If you continue to show improvement,' said Winnie, 'I might even teach you how to make my famous hedgerow wine.'

'OK, deal. Wait, does that mean I get to try some?' Rowan waggled her eyebrows.

'Absolutely not!' Winnie brayed. 'Not only are you underage but my hedgerow wine will take your mind to places it just simply isn't ready for.'

With that, the back door rattled open and Llewelyn appeared in his usual state of incredulous excitement. 'I cannot tell you the varieties I have seen this morning!' he said, his forest-eyes darting back and forth between them. Rowan sensed he was about to tell them. 'I've got hen of the woods, hedgehog fungus, stinky blusher, shaggy inkcaps. I even sourced an elven foot though it hopped halfway up the tree trunk before I could catch the bugger.'

'Wonderful, darling,' said Winnie. They kissed for several far-too-long seconds. 'Make sure you seal and label the edible ones ready for my mushroom pies. The summer fete is but a couple of weeks away.'

'Fear not,' said Llew. 'Everything will be sealed and labelled.'

But worry dashed Winnie's forehead. 'I can't afford for anything to go wrong. The fete is anticipated to be bigger than ever this year. Expectations are high.'

Winnie had already explained with great seriousness the importance of Coedyllaeth's summer fete. How she sold her famous foraged mushroom pies there every year. How everybody loved them. How there was no room for mistakes. But Rowan sensed it was more than the pressures of pastry concerning her. Since the backwards-flying birds there hadn't been any further incidents, but they had no way of knowing if it was all over, or if something else was waiting to strike.

Llew rubbed Winnie's shoulders. 'Your pies will be the talk of the town, Winnie Pooh.'

'They have to be perfect.'

'A good job you have just the man to fill your pastry.'

Rowan spluttered out a mouthful of tea. 'I'm going to go – er – fetch some more gooseberries.' She ran for the door before she had to hear any more accidental pie-based innuendoes.

'Just because your hair is as woolly as mine doesn't mean we have anything in common.' Rowan eyed the sheep. It eyed her back. She offered it some grass. Its mouth moved over her hand, soft as felt. It bleated and waited expectantly. 'More? Really? You're literally in a field of grass. OK. I get it. I get it. The grass is always greener and all that . . .'

She fed it some more and then faced the path ahead. Having completed all her tasks, Rowan had finally given in to Winnie's suggestion of going for a walk. She'd been gazing out at the view most of the summer – it was finally time to explore it. Rowan looked behind her, sure that she had already covered miles, but she could still see the distant outline of Winnie's hedge. She dithered, wondering if she ought to go back . . . surely there were more jobs to do and she had important naps to catch up on . . .

The sheep bleated.

'All right! Don't nag. I'll go for the bloody walk, but if I drown in a bog I'm holding you accountable.'

The sheep looked at her blankly. She gave it some more grass and carried on down the deserted path, stones scattering beneath her feet, sunlight breaking up the clouds overhead. It wasn't that she minded the great outdoors, it was just that . . . she didn't know how to be alone. She was used to the chaos of family life or the busy halls of St Olave's and, even when she was alone, she preferred to be absorbed in everyone else's lives online, but here, there was nobody, except—

'Me,' she said aloud. It was not reassuring.

Rowan crossed over a stile into a tall wheat field scrubbed golden by the sun, bordered by colourful scrawls of wild flowers. She could hardly believe the summer was running out. She'd spent so much of her time longing to go home but now she found herself not wanting to leave. The town was a strange place and she couldn't make sense of the inexplicable happenings or how they were connected, but even so, Coedyllaeth had become a kind of escape. She'd grown used to Winnie's strange company and she didn't want to say goodbye to her new-found friends and return to St Olave's. She hadn't realized quite how lonely she was there. Besides, there was so much still left to do. She hadn't become the person she was meant to become. She hadn't learnt to paraglide, or navigate a mountain . . . she hadn't kissed Aslyn . . . She sighed with the wind. Since the expedition, things had felt different. A camaraderie had grown between them; he seemed to listen to her more, laugh at her jokes. Perhaps there was a chance now. Perhaps she should just tell him how she felt. The thought made her want to run and hide beyond the distant mountains. What if he didn't return her feelings? What if he laughed in her face?

She distracted herself, naming the wild flowers as she passed. *Knapweed and meadow buttercup and bird's-foot trefoil.* The mud beneath her feet was sinking soft. The fields grew wilder, scruffy with grass and strewn with the great limbs of trees. *Campion and clover and mallow.* She clambered up a hill – mounds of earth hinting at an old fortress – and down the other side, through a tangle of hazels. *Ox-eye daisy and harebell and forget-me-nots.* A stream joined her, scrabbling over mossy rocks and guiding her down to the borders of a forest. Rowan walked along its swaying fringes. By daylight, it was not foreboding. Instead, its thick fabric gave way to an abundance of life – the path losing itself among plants and flowers, an old stone wall spilling over with them. *Where woods and field meet. Betwixt-places. Edges.*

Too many flowers to name now and Rowan had no words left. Her mind was flying in a hundred different directions – torn apart by the wind; splintered like the light through clouds, the light along the leaves; dispersed with the spray of birds, the colours of every single flower . . .

She felt scattered, but not less. More than herself. Lost and free.

Another, more sensible part of her mind realized that she was also quite literally lost. She looked back, but any sign of Winnie's hedge was long gone. She'd taken so many paths, so many turns. She assessed the surrounding land-scape – surely she could use it to guide her way home. The direction of the river? Or the shape of the hills? Or the pathways of birds? *Is that a thing?* She put her hand up to check the direction of the wind and had no idea what she was meant to do with the results. Then, she spotted a dot above the hill ahead of her. A kite. If there was a kite – there was a person.

The hill was spacious and grassy and easy to climb – thanks to all of her midnight cycles she was getting fitter. Somebody was sitting halfway down the slope on the other side, the kite waving about in the air above them. As Rowan approached, she realized that she recognized the person: *Gareth.*

He looked at her blankly.

She raised her hand.

The kite fell from the sky.

She ambled over, unsure. 'Hey.'

'What are you doing here?' he said, affronted, as if she'd walked into his bedroom. There were a few other kites strewn around him.

'Er, well . . . I was on a walk and I'm lost. I was about to blow my survival whistle, spell out the word SOS in sticks . . . when I saw the kite and hoped I might find a person.' Rowan smiled.

He nodded, picking up another kite and making a few adjustments. In the light, she could see how red his hair was, like one of Winnie's hedgerow poppies. It stuck out from his head as if surprised by its own colour. His face was sandy with freckles, his expression serious as ever.

'Can I sit down?' she said finally.

'I don't own the hill,' he replied, which didn't make her feel any more comfortable.

She dropped down next to him and sighed. 'Gareth, why don't you like me?'

'Oh.' He looked surprised at her comment.

'Is it because I talk too much?'

'No.'

'Is it because I'm not a local?'

'No.'

'Is it because—'

'I don't not like you.' He fiddled with the kite some more, not looking up. 'It's not you. It's me. I'm Gareth the Grump, remember?'

'I'm not sure I buy that.'

It was his turn to sigh now. 'I just – I'm not great at the social thing, at the welcoming-new-people thing. People don't tend to like me. I'm awkward.' He said it almost apologetically.

'Have you met me?' Rowan cried. 'I'm awkward. I just deal with it in the opposite way, by being too open. Too much.'

He looked up at her then. 'I like that you're like that. Probably a bit jealous of it, to be honest. I bet you're popular back at your big school in London.'

Rowan laughed. 'Mother Holle, no. Me and popularity do not go hand in hand. Don't get me wrong, I'd love to walk down the hallways and have people watch me go but that's never going to be me. The only time I'm ever talked about is when I pull off one of my frequent acts of public humiliation.'

Gareth chuckled. 'I don't see how that can be, you're friendly and chatty and interesting.'

'Interesting in a good way or in a "get her some help way" . . . ?'

'I'm serious. I like to hear your stories about your family and the Wort Cunnings, plant magic sounds fascinating.'

'You mean you've been listening to my inane babbling?'

'Well, it's hard not to hear you.'

Rowan laughed.

He turned the kite in his hands. 'I'm sorry I've been difficult. I've not been in the best of moods this summer.'

'S'OK,' Rowan shrugged. 'Is it – is it because of the happenings? They seem to have got to you.'

Gareth tensed. 'I don't want to talk about them. I'm sick of hearing about it.'

Rowan decided to change the subject. 'So, you fly kites?'

Gareth looked down at the kite. 'Well, it's a hobby. Nothing much.'

'It's cool.'

'I'm not sure about that.'

'I've never flown a kite.'

'These ones . . . well, they're not really traditional kites . . .'

'What do you mean?'

He held the kite up in the air and let go. It hovered where he'd left it. 'They don't have strings.'

'You're a telepathic kite flier? Now that *is* cool.'

'They're light. It's easy magic, but it's not really about that . . . it's . . . it's hard to explain. I like to watch them. I like to feel them. It sounds silly.'

'I have a high tolerance for silly. Can you show me?' Rowan looked at the kite eagerly.

'Sure.' Gareth's eyes moved to the kite. It soared into the air – a colourful diamond, a bright wing, the sky welcoming it with open-armed blue. It fluttered in place for a moment then dived downwards, falling almost back to the ground, then suddenly – up, up, up – riding a crest of wind until it was no more than a distant speck. It fell again but this time caught a wave of air – twisting and turning, strong and flexible as a gymnast on a mat. It performed several flips and then rolled back into a stream of ripples, warming itself in the sun.

Rowan laughed, delighted as a child. 'You're doing this with your magic?'

'I can't take all the credit. It's half my magic – half the magic of the wind. Fancy a go?'

'No, I don't. I wouldn't know how, I—'

The kite suddenly began hurtling downwards, spiralling towards the ground. Rowan's magic burst from her and stopped the kite's descent. She giggled. 'I'm doing it!' The kite nudged upwards, tentatively, and then all at once, tumbling this way and that, tangling in the air. 'I'm not sure I've got the hang of it—'

'You're trying too hard,' said Gareth. 'Let go. Let the wind do the talking.'

Rowan's Hira had always felt part of the earth, but now she loosened the roots of it, so they were there but not too tight, guiding but not gripping, spreading into the air, searching out the motions of the wind. It lifted her magic up and the kite began to flow. It sailed along a current, caught a second wave and soared upwards with a burst of daring.

Rowan began to feel it then. A beat. A rhythm. Like in band practice when all the instruments fall in sync and a song emerges from the din. There was a pattern, a living pattern, not made of hard lines but waves and eddies, curves and curlicues, like the petals of a flower but dispersed – musical notes in the air waiting to be discovered. The more she tried to understand it, the less sense it made, and so she let go, laying herself back on the ground and following the kite above as it twirled up through a funnel of air, floated along a trail of ripples, soared downwards and then caught a sudden gust that threw it upwards towards the sun. Rowan gasped, feeling the rush of air inside her, as if the whole sky were in her head. She'd never felt so weightless.

'You're good,' said Gareth.

Rowan brought the kite back to the ground. 'Beginner's luck,' she replied, breathless. 'I've never felt magic like that before.'

'It's exhilarating, isn't it?' Gareth looked at the three other kites and then they shot up in the air. He laughed, the sound pouring from him without the restraint that had held it back all summer. A flock of birds flew past in a V-shape and the kites swept upwards and joined their constellation.

'Well, now you're just showing off,' said Rowan.

Gareth chuckled and let the kites drift off in different directions.

Rowan sat back up. 'Why haven't you told the others about this?'

The kites began to sink. 'Because I don't feel the need to bang on about what language I might be or want to be. Aslyn would probably just make fun of it anyway . . .'

'I'm sure he wouldn't.'

'You don't know Aslyn.' He took the kites from the air and began to pile them together.

'How long have you guys been friends?'

Gareth looked as if didn't want to talk about it. 'Since we were young. We've always spent the summer together, getting up to no good. We used to be close, inseparable, and then we grew up and things got more . . . complicated. Last summer and this summer, he's changed. He prances about in that bloody multicoloured coat. You know Laila bought it for him?'

'Really?'

'Told him it looked like the kaleidoscopic colours of the Astral witches, so obviously he never takes it off. It's like – like he's suddenly too good for this place. Too good for everyone here. Too good for me.' Gareth turned his head back up to the sky, his voice heavy against it. 'He and Laila spend all their time lost in dreams. They miss the beauty here.'

'I'm sure if you spoke to him he'd understand—'

'He'll never understand,' said Gareth, back to his old abruptness. 'It doesn't matter.'

'He might.'

'You're just saying that because you think the sun shines out of his ar—'

'Gareth! I do not!'

'You like him, don't you?'

'What?' Rowan cried. 'Me? *Moi*? You think I like Aslyn?' Her laugh came out almost as high pitched as Winnie's. 'Why would you think that – that's completely – OK. FINE. I like Aslyn. Is it that obvious?'

'Yes.'

'Oh Goddess.' Rowan buried her head in her hands. 'It's not like I'm going to do anything about it. It's just a stupid, marginally obsessive crush.'

'Probably best to leave it that way with Aslyn.'

Rowan looked at him, trying to work out why he had such an issue with Aslyn. 'Do you . . . like Laila?'

'No.' Gareth shook his head, laughing. 'Not my type. You should be careful with her, you know, or she'll end up pulling you into her dream world.'

'I like Laila's dream world.'

He grumbled something inaudible. They sat in silence for a while, watching the clouds stirring the air above them.

'I don't want to go back,' said Rowan.

'Back home?'

'No. Back to reality. Back to school. It's been nice having people to hang out with, even if Coedyllaeth is a weird place.'

'Maybe you just need to find your people.'

'What if I don't have people? What if I'm just . . . an outsider?'

'Then find some other outsiders,' Gareth replied matter-of-factly. 'Are there no witches at your school?'

'I don't think so. Maybe one girl . . . I get a feeling . . . but, she pretty much keeps herself to herself. I don't think she'd want me harassing her.'

'You could try talking to her instead.'

Rowan laughed. 'It's a fine line when it comes to me.'

'True.' He gathered his kites, layering them together carefully. 'Anyway, I've got to head. Got to help my mum bake cakes.'

'Kite flying and cake baking. What other secret skills do you have?'

'I'm mainly testing the cakes – Mum is trying out recipes for the summer fete.'

'I've heard a lot about this fete. Does the whole town revolve around it?'

'Pretty much.' Gareth stood up, brushing the grass off his legs. 'Us provincial types have to have something to look forward to.' He smiled. 'See you soon, Rowan.'

'Bye, Gareth.'

Rowan watched him walk away and only when he was halfway down the hill did she remember that she was lost and stranded. She jumped up and ran after him.

'Wait, Gareth! Wait for meeeee!'

RED SKY AT MORNING

'Faster!' Laila hollered. 'Faster!'

They'd met at the local park which was always empty by night. A cluster of swings. A climbing frame and slide. Two spring rocking horses. A metal roundabout, which Laila had lain herself across, arms stretched out beyond her head. The boys were spinning it round and round with their magic.

'Faster!' Her hair trailed on the asphalt. 'Come and join, Rowan!'

'I'm good.' Rowan wanted to but she held back, ignoring the familiar feeling of being left out. There was just too much opportunity for embarrassment – what if their magic couldn't manage her extra weight?

The roundabout began to slow.

'What are you doing?' said Laila.

'My magic is tired,' Gareth responded. 'And you'll be sick.'

'I won't.'

'You said that on the waltzers when the funfair came to town last year and what happened?'

Laila giggled. 'I threw up.'

'Where?'

'On you.'

'And me,' Aslyn added.

The three of them laughed at the shared memory. Rowan joined in.

'You don't know when to stop,' said Gareth.

'When I've had enough fun?' Laila giggled. They sat down in the centre of the playground, catching their breath. 'Speaking of,' Laila continued. 'I have a new suspect. A witch I've never seen before came to see my mum the other day about some of her plants. I eavesdropped on their conversation. She's a Runic Witch. They're powerful and she's spending the summer in Coedyllaeth, which means she arrived when the happenings started . . .'

'And?' said Rowan.

Laila shrugged. 'That's all I've got so far, but I think we need to consider her.'

'How many people are we considering now?' Gareth replied. 'You've suspected most of the town.'

Laila glared. 'We're getting close. I can feel it.'

Rowan wasn't sure she agreed. They seemed more lost than they'd ever been. 'Winnie's spent the entire week obsessively measuring the height of her puff pastry toppings in preparation for the fete. I know she's worried something might happen there with so many people gathered together.'

'Well, she's right,' said Laila. 'Anything could happen.'

'I hope not,' Rowan replied. 'She really cares about this town. It's, like, her . . . refuge. She's even mentioned escalating things if the events continue, calling on some other groves for backup.'

'Really?' Aslyn scoffed. 'That seems a bit of an overreaction. Who actually cares about this town except the people in it?'

'Well, the people in it are people too,' said Gareth, coldly.

'Don't you ever wonder why we have to keep things so hidden?' said Laila. 'Why we can't just let our magic free, bring the light of the moon into the light of day. Cowans would love us. We'd be revered.'

Gareth shrugged despondently. 'Unfortunately, I'm not sure it would be quite so smooth, Laila.'

'I've heard in London there are places where cowans and witches mix and magic is performed openly. We're a new generation, things are changing – we shouldn't be afraid to be who we are.'

'You could make them all a dress of rainbows,' Aslyn mocked. 'Or end up lynched like Black Annis . . .'

Laila pouted, but perked up at the mention of Black Annis. 'I still think Black Annis might be behind this whole thing you know.'

Rowan shivered at the thought, remembering the derelict cottage. She never wanted to go back there.

'So your main suspect isn't even real?' Gareth replied, flatly. 'Nothing more than a legend.'

'There's moon-truth at the heart of all legends,' Laila countered. 'You know we could just ask her ourselves . . .'

Rowan looked at Laila. 'What?'

'I heard if you say her name three times she appears before you.' Laila smiled slowly. An empty smile. 'Maybe I should do it . . .'

Rowan's shiver took flight. She searched the darkness around them, feeling suddenly exposed, as if someone were watching them – had been watching them all along. The park was motionless, the apparatus warped by shadows.

Laila cleared her throat. The words came out as a whisper: 'Black Annis.'

Louder: 'Black Annis.'

She took a deep breath, glancing between them with trembling eyes: 'BLACK ANNIS.'

For a moment there was only silence and then—

A swing creaked behind Laila, moving suddenly. The

roundabout screeched with rust, starting to spin. The spring rocking horses followed, nodding back and forth. Laila screamed. Aslyn jumped up. 'What the hell—'

Gareth fell back laughing.

Aslyn narrowed his eyes at him. 'Is this you?'

'You should have seen the look on your faces . . .' Gareth snorted, a hand over his mouth.

'Gareth!' Laila yelled. 'I almost had a heart attack!'

'Serves you right,' he retorted. 'Getting so carried away.'

'I wasn't scared.' Aslyn shrugged. 'Just . . . confused.'

Gareth chuckled. 'You looked scared to me.'

'Well, I was bloody terrified,' Rowan cried, making everyone laugh.

'Come on,' said Laila. 'Let's get out of here. Go to the stones.'

They left the abandoned playground and made their way through town. As they climbed up the hill, Rowan recounted the latest story of Winnie's antics to lighten the mood. She'd had more friends over the night before and Rowan had found them all dancing around the garden in the early hours. 'They were making these weird sounds,' Rowan described. 'Like deranged owls.' They all laughed, including Aslyn. Rowan felt bad using Winnie as entertainment but it made him take notice of her. 'I'm pretty sure I saw one of them dancing in the wheelbarrow—'

'Wait,' said Laila. 'Maybe it's your aunt!'

'What?'

'Maybe she's behind the strange happenings, performing secret rituals right under your nose.'

Rowan shook her head emphatically. 'No. It's just Winnie and her eccentric friends communing with plants and being generally crazy. Welcome to the world of the Wort Cunnings.'

'But you said she's been making you work all summer. Maybe she's been using you without your knowledge, getting you to prepare all these ingredients for their nefarious rituals?'

Rowan tried to follow Laila's line of reasoning but it was spinning out of control.

'No, she makes medicines and magical ingredients. They were probably just drunk on hedgerow wine, apparently that stuff does weird things to you . . .'

'Really?' said Laila, distracted. 'Can you swipe us some? We should test it.'

'Test it,' Gareth repeated. 'You just want to get drunk.'

'There's no way I can get any,' said Rowan. 'Winnie has everything categorized and labelled. She'd know it was missing.'

'Well, at least try,' Laila encouraged.

'Sure,' Rowan replied, mainly to appease her.

They reached the top of the hill and looked out over the town – above, the sky was dark but a ring of red sat along the horizon, as if the mountains had punctured the sun on its descent.

'Beautiful,' Laila whispered. 'I bet I could make a dress out of that.'

'Red sky at night, witches' delight,' said Rowan.

Aslyn laid himself on the ground among the stones, in his usual reclined position. 'Red sky at morning, hunters' warning. Isn't that how it goes?'

'Red sky at night, witches' delight. Red sky at morning, hunters' warning. Smoke in the sky, you'd better get hiding,' Gareth recited.

'Why are all the old songs so unsettling?' said Laila.

'Because people like you probably made them up,' he replied.

Laila made a face and sat down beside them, stretching out. 'I can't believe the summer is coming to an end. I wish it could go on forever. And, Aslyn . . . Rowan . . . neither of you will even be back here next year.'

'I'm so out of here,' said Aslyn, then, at the look on Laila's face he added, 'But you guys can come to mine in Hampshire.

You can get a train into London from there, Laila. We'll be old enough to sneak into bars and stuff.'

Laila's eyes widened. 'Can you imagine?'

'It'll be fun. You should all come.'

'And me?' Rowan asked. She hadn't meant to say it out loud.

He nodded at her. 'Sure. We can hang.'

Her heart swelled. *We can hang. Three perfect words.* Her thoughts ran ahead of her – Hampshire and Forest Hill weren't a million miles apart – they could visit each other before the summer . . . if they started going out they could meet halfway on the weekends. She'd have a boyfriend outside of school which was so much cooler than going out with someone in school. *He's in a band,* she would say casually—

She felt a rush run through her, like the kite soaring into the sky. She needed to tell him how she felt. She'd witnessed a moon garden, sneaked out to magical stones, flown a kite with her mind, battled an almighty hedge – surely she could tell a guy she had a crush on him. *What do I have to lose except my dignity? She'd never needed that anyway.*

The night wore on, Laila steering the conversation this way and that, round and round; the stars rolling over the clouds, the moon stretching itself back to fullness in the sky. Eventually, Laila picked herself up. 'I better get back. Mum's going to be out in the garden tonight.'

'I've got to head too,' said Gareth.

This was the point that Rowan always joined them, but she bit her tongue. Aslyn always stayed behind, and she was going to stay too. 'I'm – er – going to chill a bit longer.' She tried to sound casual.

Gareth raised his eyebrows at her.

'Oh,' said Laila, giving Aslyn a sideways look. 'Are you sure? I can walk you back to the bikes.'

'I know the way.'

'I've got more theories to discuss with you.'

'Tell me next time.'

'Er – OK then.' Laila still sounded unsure. 'Well, don't forget to try and get some of the hedgerow wine for us, it'll be fun!'

'I'll do my best,' said Rowan.

Rowan watched Laila and Gareth walk away. Silence fell. She turned to Aslyn with a smile, rapidly regretting her decision. The butterflies in her stomach scattered and hid. 'So—' She tried to think of something to say. 'How come you always stay out here?'

Aslyn looked up. 'What?'

'You know, out here with the stones?'

He shrugged. 'I like to stargaze. There are like . . . lots of stars.'

'Yeah.' Rowan nodded. He appeared to have nothing else to add. 'So – er – are you going to this fete, then?'

'Probably not. It's lame.'

'You mean you're not performing in the local morris dance?'

Aslyn snorted. 'Not my bag. I was dragged along to the fete last year, but got in trouble.'

'Why?'

'Laila, Gareth and I used magic to beat the coconut shy over and over again. We cleared out all its prizes. Until my dad found out.' He laughed at the memory, sitting up. They were side by side, close enough to touch. 'You going?'

Rowan looked up at him. Did he want her to go? 'I have to help Winnie out, so I'll be there . . . yeah. You should come and try her mushroom pies, apparently they're irresistible.'

'Don't really like mushrooms.'

'Oh—'

'But maybe I'll come.'

Their eyes met and Rowan's courage fled. She looked away and noticed something glinting beneath his jacket. A necklace.

He brushed a hand through his hair distractedly and she caught another glimpse of it – she recognized its moon pendant.

'Laila's necklace . . .' she whispered.

It took him a moment to realize what she was referring to. 'Oh—' He looked down at it, slightly flustered, and pulled his jacket shut. 'Yeah, I borrowed it.'

'You borrowed Laila's necklace?' Rowan replied, confused. The words came out before she could stop them. 'Are you and Laila . . . together?'

'What?' said Aslyn, shaking his head. 'No. We've been friends since we were kids. We're just mates.'

'Really?'

'Yeah, really.' He shrugged. 'Why?'

Rowan took a breath, her heart flipping. There would be no better moment. 'Because, I like you.'

The silence that followed might have been only a few seconds but it felt excruciatingly long.

'Oh,' he said eventually, which was not the response she'd been hoping for. 'Huh.'

Huh? Huh! Huh was almost worse than laughter.

Rowan stuttered. 'I just wanted you to know before the end of summer, in case—'

'Thanks,' he interrupted. 'You're cool, Rowan, but, yeah, I don't really see you in that way. I actually have something going with someone else. A girl back home. Like, we're not official or anything, but we're a thing. She's in the band.'

Rowan nodded. The butterflies in her stomach burst into painful flames. The stars fell down to earth with a shatter. She wanted to dig up one of the stones and bury herself in the hole left there. 'The band. I see. That's cool. She sounds cool. I – er – you know, I think I have to get back actually. Winnie needs me, vinegars need turning, you know how it is.' She stood up, stumbling a little. 'There I go again.' She laughed. 'Right, well, bye, Aslyn. Sorry. Bye.'

'See ya.' He saluted her.

She ran. Halfway down the hill she turned back and could see he'd lain back down in the circle of stones.

Rowan found the bike in the park where she'd left it. She cycled back home, faster than she'd ever cycled before, not veering once. She hoped she could somehow outrun the devastation of her embarrassment but it chased her like a rapacious hedge troll. When she got back, she hid the bike and sneaked through the back door – but the light in the kitchen clicked on.

Winnie was sitting at the table.

Rowan gasped.

They stared at each other.

Winnie bristled. 'Where on earth have you been?'

Rowan couldn't face this discussion now. She already felt as if she were going to burst. She just wanted to run to her bed and hide. 'Just out,' she snapped, moving towards the door.

Winnie looked taken aback. 'That is not an appropriate response.'

'I was out with friends. Laila and others. I didn't want to worry you.'

'Well, you have achieved the exact opposite of that. Why didn't you ask me?'

'Because . . .' Rowan couldn't find an excuse. 'You're not my mum!'

Winnie's big eyes blinked. 'You're in my care and trust – and I trusted you.' The disappointment in her voice made it worse.

The words rose up now and Rowan couldn't stop them. 'Can you blame me? I work non-stop for you all day. I do my best to learn everything even while the bloody hedge thorns me and there's nothing to do here! I'm bored! I'm young! Why shouldn't I be out having fun? It's what everybody else does!'

'And you wish to be like everybody else?' said Winnie.

'YES!' Rowan cried. 'Sometimes I'd rather be anyone but myself. You might be content with your whole world being a hedge, but maybe that's not what I want. Maybe I don't want to be a Hedge Witch. Maybe I don't want to be a Wort Cunning at all! Did anyone ever think to ask *me*?'

Winnie sat still. 'If you think my whole world is a hedge, you've missed the entire point of everything.'

'Well, that does sound like me,' said Rowan, tears pricking at her eyes.

'Why are you hiding from yourself, Rowan?'

'Me hiding?' Rowan exploded. 'I'm not the one living behind a ten-foot hedge! You act as if you know everything, as if you're not afraid of anything but you are – you're scared, you're terrified of this town rejecting you! It's why you're so bothered about these happenings!'

Rowan couldn't bear the look on Winnie's face. She ran from it. Out of the door. Up the stairs. Into her room. She stopped in front of the mirror, seeing all of her flaws – but she'd always liked the person beneath them. Until now. She dived into bed and let go of the tears she'd been holding back. They came thick and fast, her stomach twisting with humiliation and shame and guilt heavy as bad pastry. She saw herself in Aslyn's eyes and wanted to disappear from herself. What had she been thinking? That he would actually like *her?* A silly, robust, coordinationally challenged Plant Witch. Someone to laugh with, and *at*. Not someone to kiss. She saw herself in Winnie's eyes and felt worse. An owl pealed a lonely sound somewhere. She wanted to go home. She wanted to call her mum and tell her she wanted to go home. She pulled out her phone but couldn't bring herself to dial the number. She couldn't take her mum's disappointment on top of Winnie's. She needed to fix this herself – she just didn't know how.

She wiped her tears away. She knew what her mum would say, she could hear her voice now: *The morning is always wiser than the evening.* Rowan hoped so. She turned over and waited for sleep to come, the night sounds fitful beyond her window.

She couldn't say when she'd drifted off, nor what time it was when she woke. Winnie hadn't come to wake her. Memories of the night before came like a gut punch. She rolled over with a groan. The light fell onto her pillow, a pinkish hue. Rowan frowned. *Pink?* She looked up, out of the window, and tried to make sense of the sky.

It was red. Not the soft red of dawn. Not the red of fire or dust clouds. But a bright, bold, absurd red. An impossible red.

Rowan bolted upright, everything suddenly falling into place.

It's them! They were the ones doing it!

Rowan watched Winnie from the kitchen window. She was wrenching long stems from the hedge with great and tender force. The sky above had turned back to blue, although Rowan could see a russet hue still lingering about the clouds. She poured hot water over the herbs and sighed, wishing she could wash away everything she'd said last night. She'd stayed out of the way all morning, listening to Winnie panicking downstairs.

'The sky is red, Llewelyn! Red! It's red! Red. Red. Red.'

'I can see that, Winnie Pooh.'

'Skies are not meant to be red! Traditionally – they're blue!'

'I know that, Winnie Pooh. Calm down now.'

Rowan could hear her on the phone discussing the situation. 'It's one incident too many now! The cowans are disturbed! Their minds can't handle this level of impossibility.'

Rowan thought about offering up her theory but she didn't know for sure if she was right. She wanted to find out for herself first. Winnie had enough on her plate . . . and she had to give them a chance . . . *didn't she?* The benefit of the doubt. She shook her head feeling like more of an idiot than ever before. *Was it really them?*

Rowan nodded to her own reflection, picked up the tea, and went outside.

'Aunt Winnie.'

Winnie turned around. Rowan had thought she might be angry to see her, but she just looked weary, which made it worse.

'I made you some tea. It's my own recipe, my favourite herbs for cheering. I thought you might want to take a break?'

Winnie stood defensively, head raised, shears in hand, but then she dropped them down. 'To the kitchen then.'

They sat down at the table, instruments bubbling and ticking; extracting magic from every root, stem, and leaf. Rowan nudged the tea towards Winnie.

'I'm so sorry, Winnie—'

'I'm sorry, Rowan—'

They said it at the same time.

'Why would you be sorry?' Rowan exclaimed. 'I'm the one who sneaked out and lied and said terrible things that I didn't mean.' She looked at Winnie, ashamed. 'I really didn't mean them.'

'Yes, but I'm looking after you. So anything you do wrong is something I've done wrong. Your mother has put her trust in me.'

'No.' Rowan shook her head. 'No way. You haven't done anything wrong. You've been brilliant—'

'Hedgecraft is tough and I went too big, too soon. I'm a pusher and I pushed too hard—'

'No. I've loved it. Really. I know I've moaned and grumbled and made a hundred mistakes but I've never learnt so much in my life and I like that you push me, that you think I'm . . . capable.'

'Of course you're capable!' said Winnie, fiercely. 'You're resilient, resourceful and—'

'Robust?'

'I was going to say radiant. As radiant as a rowan berry.'

Rowan looked down, shaking her head. 'But I'm not . . .' She traced a stain on the table. 'I was upset last night because I told a boy I liked him. And he . . . it wasn't like he laughed or anything, but I could see it in his face, that the thought of me, in *that* way, that it had never even occurred to him.'

'Well.' Winnie's chins snapped together. 'If he can't see how brilliant you are then he has an entirely empty head.'

'He doesn't—' Rowan stopped. 'Actually, to be honest, he is a bit of an idiot.'

'I thought you liked this boy.'

'I do – I . . .' Rowan sighed, rolling her eyes at herself. 'I honestly don't really know him. I just got lost somewhere in my fantasy world – it's a very extensive world. The idea of a summer fling. The thought of going back to school and not being a complete loser, for once.'

Winnie's eyes softened sadly. 'You really think that?'

Rowan shrugged. 'Doesn't really matter what I think if it's what the world thinks of me.'

'On the contrary, the only thing that matters is what you think of yourself.'

'But you're – you. You're so sure of yourself. You don't give a damn what the rest of the world thinks.'

'Don't swear, Rowan.'

'Sorry.'

'Did I ever tell you the story of my first kiss?'

Rowan looked up, intrigued. 'No. But I have to hear this.'

Winnie took a sip of tea. 'I wasn't much past your age. It was a boy from school. At the time I thought he was the bee's begonias but honestly I can't even remember his name. Anyway, afterwards, because I was tall and *robust*, he told everyone that it had been like kissing a man. I was a laughing stock for weeks.' Winnie spoke matter-of-factly.

'He sounds charming.'

'Such is life. I didn't exactly fit in at school. Bigger than half the boys, with a wandering eye and a strange interest in shrubbery did not exactly win me favour. I carried that shame with me for a long time. But eventually, I decided to wear a different hat. To be proud of who I am, the rest of the world be damned.'

'Winnie! You swore!'

'Well, sometimes swearing is necessary to emphasize a point.' She grinned.

Rowan smiled but it fell away. 'How do you do it? How do you get rid of all the shame?'

'That's a big question, Rowan, and, contrary to what you think, I don't have all the answers. But, I would say that you have to learn it, and it takes time, and it's hard, and you'll be knocked back many times, but like a great hedge – the more it is cut back, the more it rises higher and stronger!'

'You're one heck of a hedge, Winnie.'

'Thank you, Rowan.' Winnie nodded. 'But – you were right last night.' She looked out of the window, her strong mast of a jaw wobbling in a way Rowan had never seen. 'This town is my home, but it's become my hiding place too. I still have some growing to do.'

Rowan smiled. 'Maybe you need a bigger hat.'

'Indeed.'

They shared a laugh.

'And, Winnie, I didn't mean what I said,' said Rowan. 'About Wort Cunning magic being boring. I know it's not.'

'Of course it's not,' Winnie replied. 'After all, we grow magic. There are other languages out there that sound more exciting, that promise all sorts of flightly delights, but we are the roots. Never forget that. It's perfectly understandable that you don't yet know what you're going to grow into. Not everybody knows from a young age.'

'Did you?'

'Well . . . yes.'

Rowan was not encouraged. 'What if I have nothing to grow into? What if I'm never going to find my way?'

'Nonsense. I know that someday when you find the magic waiting for you it's going to be spectacular.'

Rowan looked up at Winnie, at the intensity in her strange, bright eyes, and believed perhaps that it could be possible. Winnie's gaze moved somewhere far away. 'And if I'd ever been lucky enough to have a daughter,' she said, swallowing a lump in her long neck, 'I – I'd like her to have been just like you.'

Rowan didn't know what to say; her throat felt thick. 'Maybe a bit more reliable though . . .'

'No. Just as you are.'

This time, Rowan said nothing. Winnie wiped at her wandering eye. They finished their teas in the pleasant gurgling of the kitchen.

Afterwards, Rowan washed up the mugs at the sink and turned back to Winnie. 'I have one last request and I don't think you're going to like it.'

Winnie's eyes snapped back into their shrewd setting. 'Yes?'

'My friends are meeting up in two nights' time. Could I go? It's the last time and there's something I need to do. I promise I'll only be an hour. I'll be back before eleven.'

Winnie considered her words, then nodded. 'You may go.'

'Really?' Rowan hadn't expected that.

'If you'd asked me at the start of the summer I'd have let you go – with a curfew, of course.'

'But it's at night!'

'What kind of a witch would you be if you didn't go out after dark?'

Rowan laughed. 'You know, you're pretty cool, Winnie.'

'I'm aware. But, Rowan, do be careful. With everything going on . . . I know, I know, I've had my own reasons for being concerned about these events, but what's been happening goes beyond me. Magic is a careful balance and we should never take that for granted. The magical world is a wonderful one but the scales can tip like that.' Winnie clicked her fingers.

'Black Annis . . .' said Rowan, thinking of the legend, how the town turned on her.

'What?'

'The old town legend, about a woman who was killed here for being a witch.'

'I don't know about that but I can assure you that over time there have been thousands of Black Annises.'

Rowan's face fell.

'I'm not trying to scare you. I'm just reminding you that as witches, hats aside, we must always keep a part of ourselves hidden. That's just good sense.'

Rowan nodded. 'I'll be careful.'

'You'll also be home at eleven and not a moment later, otherwise you'll be spending your last days of summer de-snailing the hedge.'

'Noted.'

BEYOND THE HEDGE

Rowan cycled up to the top of the hill without getting off the bike. She arrived, entirely out of breath, but at least she had accomplished something this summer.

The others were already there. Laila looked up and smiled. 'Rowan—'

Rowan strode forwards. 'Is it you?' The words had been in her mouth since she left the house. 'Are you the ones behind the happenings?'

Gareth and Aslyn's heads jerked up.

Laila frowned. 'Of course not. You know we'd never be powerful enough for that kind of magic. I have some new theories though . . .'

'How about hearing my theory?' Rowan rebutted.

Laila opened her mouth, then shut it. 'OK.'

Rowan moved forwards into the centre of the stones. 'I agree – you're not powerful enough, but you have help.' She patted one of the stones. 'The stones. You're casting the spell inside them.' She pointed at Aslyn. 'He's casting the spell inside them.'

Aslyn sat up from where he'd been lolling.

'Red sky at night . . .' Rowan circled the stone. 'We'd been discussing it. Then the next morning the sky is red. Seems kind of a coincidence, doesn't it? Or maybe you dreamed about a red sky that night after we talked about it?'

Aslyn's eyes shifted.

'You always stay after the rest of us leave. You're sleeping here at night, aren't you? You're practising dream magic – your dreams are somehow seeping into the town. It's why the events are all so weird . . . And the stones are amplifying the magic – giving it power. You wouldn't be able to do it without them. Laila's necklace too – you're adding an extra kick to the magic with lunar water.'

'Er – no – er . . .' Aslyn gulped at the air.

Rowan turned to Laila, who'd stood up. Her smile bloomed slowly. 'Busted.' She put up her hands. 'You're good Rowan. I'm impressed.'

'So I'm right?' Rowan replied, not wanting to believe it. 'It is you guys?'

Laila shrugged innocently. 'It was just meant to be a bit of fun.'

'But – but all your theories!' Rowan cried. 'All the endless discussions of who's behind it!'

'All part of the fun.' She grabbed Rowan's hands, contrite. 'Are you mad? Oh, please don't be mad. I'm sorry we didn't tell you—'

Rowan pulled away, taking a few steps back. 'So you've been lying to me all this time?'

'Not lying, just not revealing the whole light-of-day truth. It's just you're an outsider and—'

'Outsider,' Rowan repeated, her heart sinking.

'We thought you might tell your aunt,' said Aslyn, coming over, stumbling on a stone. 'You're not going to, are you? Tell your aunt? My parents would kill me. Please don't tell her. You're one of us, part of the gang.' He touched her on the arm, looked into her eyes. 'It would really mean so much to me.'

Rowan ignored him and turned to Gareth. 'You knew?'

He sighed. 'Yeah, I knew, but I've been against it the whole summer. I've told these two they're being idiots, that dream magic isn't something to be messed with, but I don't get listened to . . .'

'It wasn't my idea.' Aslyn pointed at Laila. 'Laila made me do it! She went on and on about it, saying we had to do something big with our last summer here. She's very good at nagging—'

'Aslyn, you're such an ass!' Laila yelled. 'You can't pin this all on me – they are *your* dreams after all. You know you were excited to test out your magic!' She swivelled back to Rowan. 'We were just bored. Something to keep us entertained. Or me.' She laughed her hollow laugh. 'And we're only going to do it one last time . . .'

'The summer fete.' Rowan took a step back. 'Tomorrow.'

Laila nodded. 'Everyone together . . . it's too tempting!'

'That's exactly why you shouldn't do it!' said Gareth. 'What if it goes wrong? Astral Witches are experts. They have complete control over their dreams. Your spell simply causes Aslyn's dreams to enter reality and you have no idea what he'll dream or how much of it will become true. What if he has a nightmare?'

'I won't,' Aslyn replied archly. 'I know what I'm doing.'

'You have no idea what you're doing! It doesn't even work most of the time, it's completely random—'

'I'm gaining more control,' said Aslyn.

'You're gaining more ego!'

'You're just jealous of me, like always.'

Gareth went quiet, looking away. He seemed to shrink into himself.

'Oh, Gareth, don't be a grump,' said Laila. 'Aslyn will be gone next year, this is our last bit of fun. Nothing we've done has caused any real harm. It's just one last time before the summer's over and we have to return to normality . . .'

'I'm not doing it again if Rowan's going to tell her aunt,' said Aslyn. He turned to Rowan with a pleading expression. 'You're not going to, are you?'

Rowan looked between them all, wondering how she'd considered them friends, and then, she laughed. 'That old bat? Of course I'm not going to tell her! She'd probably come at you all with hedge cutters.'

Aslyn laughed, still unsure. 'Really?'

'I'm one of you guys.'

Laila beamed. 'Of course you are.'

'I was just annoyed you guys didn't tell me, that's all,' said Rowan. 'But I'm in. Let's do it. Let's turn this town upside down. I mean, don't literally do that, that might be going a bit far . . .'

'Well, I'm out,' Gareth growled, standing up. 'I'm not going to sit around while another one of you joins in this lunacy.' He stalked past them, shaking his head at Rowan. 'I thought you had more sense.'

'Maybe she's just more fun than you!' Aslyn shouted after him.

'Gareth!' Laila called. 'Gareth, don't be like that. Come back—'

But he didn't stop.

She turned around with a sigh. 'He takes everything way too seriously. I knew you'd understand, Rowan.'

'Of course. And look what I managed to steal—' Rowan rummaged in her rucksack and pulled out a bottle of wine.

'The hedgerow wine!' Laila twirled. 'Yes! Yes!'

Rowan opened it. 'This will definitely stir up Aslyn's dreams.'

They sat down in the circle of stones and passed the wine around between them. Laila seemed excited that Rowan knew what was going on. She talked her through it all, how they'd pulled it off. Aslyn discussed his growing propensity for dream magic, how he was beginning to become self-aware in dreams. Rowan nodded eagerly, looking more impressed than ever.

It wasn't long before they both fell asleep. Deeply asleep.

Rowan called their names, poked them a few times but they were both snoring away. She stood up and began to drag them out of the circle of stones. It wasn't easy.

'Rowan—'

'Bloody Holle!' She leapt at the voice. 'Gareth. Why are you back?'

'I don't know. I decided to come back to try and convince you idiots out of it, but . . . what are you doing?'

It was Rowan's turn to look guilty now. 'I drugged them.' She held up the bottle of hedgerow wine.

'You what?!'

'It's not hedgerow wine. It's just watered-down red wine with three drops of Winnie's valerian root tincture. Sends you into a deep sleep. A happy one, if that helps. They'll be out till the early hours and I figured if I moved them beyond the circle of stones then the spell won't work. They won't be able to disrupt the fete tomorrow.'

Gareth stared at her blankly for a moment, and then he smiled. 'Well, you're no idiot.'

'I don't know about that,' said Rowan, looking at the sleeping Aslyn and Laila, thinking how blind she'd been. 'But I have my moments.'

'Why didn't you just tell your aunt?'

'I wanted to be sure you guys were behind it before I made wild accusations. But believe me, after the fete I'll be telling her the truth.'

Gareth nodded towards Aslyn and Laila. 'They won't be happy about that.'

Rowan shrugged. 'I was always the outsider anyway.' She shook off the hurt of it. 'So, are you going to help me?'

'Of course.'

Once they were done, Rowan took blankets out of her bag and put them over Laila and Aslyn. Gareth shook his head.

'What? I don't want them getting cold,' she said.

Rowan came to stand next to him at the edge of the stones, the town below them. 'We saved the village fete!' She whooped and they exchanged a smile. 'Is it normal to be so invested in a village fete?'

Gareth chuckled. 'This place will do weird things to you.'

Rowan took the last batch of pies out of the oven to cool. They'd been in for exactly twenty-two minutes and forty-five seconds, which was the time that Winnie had resolved created the perfect amount of puff. Winnie came in, in a bright orange sundress and a large hat with half a hedgerow attached to it. She took out a ruler and measured the height of each pie. 'Marvellous. They look good, don't they?'

'Good enough to eat.'

Winnie glanced out of the window. 'No strange occurrences this morning?'

Rowan shook her head confidently. 'Absolutely nothing. It's all going to be fine, Winnie.'

'Yes.' Winnie nodded. 'Yes. Yes. I bought you something . . .'

'Oh.'

Winnie bustled out of the door and returned with a wide-brimmed straw hat as large as her own, decorated decadently with rowan berries.

'Errrr – wow.' Rowan tried to sound pleased. 'That is . . . a lot to take in . . .'

'Do you like it?'

'I . . . do.'

'I thought we could be matching to go to the fete today.'

'What a good idea. I'll go get ready.'

'Wear something bright!'

Rowan finished getting herself ready upstairs. She put the hat on in the mirror and it was official – she now looked as cuckoo as Winnie. She wondered if she could throw it out of the window and claim a sudden breeze had carried it off . . . but she knew there was no hope. She laughed and considered her gravestone:

Rowan Greenfinch: Died, Not With Cats, But Hats. Mad. Alone. But Utterly Radiant.

She'd take it.

She skipped downstairs, but when she went into the kitchen she immediately sensed something was wrong. Something was different.

No. No. No . . .

She turned three-sixty, trying to identify what it was. She went to the window and looked out at the view, searching for any abnormalities along the horizon. Sunlight streamed over the hills and into the kitchen, filling it with light. A beautiful view . . . *a view? There's a view! The hedge . . .*

'The hedge is gone!' she cried.

'Not gone,' said Winnie, coming into the room. 'Just rearranged.'

'Rearranged?!'

'I thought it was time to open up the front of the house a bit. I don't think I need a hedge the whole way around – I've extended it out at the back instead.'

Rowan's mouth dropped. 'You've moved the hedge?'

'Well, mostly it moved itself, but I oversaw the operation.'

Rowan laughed and turned back to the window. 'Well, I like it. A nice view from the sink.'

'I thought so. Don't know why I didn't do it years ago.'

They grinned at each other and then began to load the pies together ready for the car.

The fete was held at the bottom of town. It was bigger than Rowan had expected – a fanfare of flags zigzagged back and forth across the field, rows of stalls, a mini circus tent, a bandstand and, at the far end, a large hot-air balloon nodding its head in the wind. The sky above was clear, the kind of blue that summer days dream of.

Rowan and Winnie made their way to the stall to get set up. They passed the coconut shy where a man was balancing the coconuts in preparation. Rowan thought of Laila and Aslyn. They would have woken up by now and she was sure she wasn't their favourite person in the world. *Would they show?* She didn't think so. Aslyn would definitely be in hiding. Rowan realized she wasn't that bothered if she saw him again, but Laila . . .

'Rowan! Why are you staring at coconuts! The clock is ticking!' Winnie harried. 'We have much to do!'

'Coming, Winnie Pooh!'

'If you call me that in public I shall call you Sorbus!'

'Point taken.'

Before long they were busy putting out the pies, preparing the signs and the display. 'The fete starts at one,' Winnie explained. 'But we won't open until two to make sure the crowds are really hungry. Be ready.'

'Hedge ready.' Rowan saluted.

The field began to swell with bodies, children running ahead of parents, trying to take everything in at once. Rowan had never seen so many people in the town, drawn out of hiding by the bright beacon of the fete, like shoals of fish from nooks in the rocks. The band started up, a sprightly fiddle rousing the atmosphere. The sun glistened above and the scent of candyfloss floated through the air. A gymnastics display was announced in the centre of the field, to be followed by a dog show. The hot-air balloon had started offering rides, swaying into the air, tethered by a rope so it couldn't rise above the treeline. Rowan found herself smiling, taking in the scene, wondering how she could ever have thought Coedyllaeth a glum and lonely place.

At two o'clock, Winnie turned to her with great solemnity. 'It's time.'

They opened the stall and were soon overwhelmed with a queue stretching right around the field. Rowan didn't even have time to be embarrassed by the ridiculousness of their matching hats as she rushed to serve customers, restock the pies, keep up with Winnie's string of orders. The crowds ate the pies with relish.

'Every year I come here,' growled Emlyn, the man with the eye patch. 'And every year, I forget how bloody delicious these pies are. The pastry is as rich as a good man's soul and lighter than a breeze in spring.'

'Thank you, Emlyn. No need to swear.'

'Sorry, Winifred.'

Llewelyn arrived just before three. 'Is she keeping you busy?'

'Just a bit,' Rowan breathed, handing someone change. 'But it's going well.'

'Of course it is. I foraged these mushrooms.' He winked. 'If you want to go and have a look around, I can take over for a bit.'

'Really?' said Rowan. 'That OK, Winnie?'

'He's not as efficient as you, but we'll make do.' Winnie smiled. 'Go on, go have fun.'

Rowan wandered into the crowds. She looked around for Gareth, hoping that at least he might have shown, but she couldn't see him. She didn't know anyone else, but the atmosphere was friendly. She stopped to pet some donkeys, had several goes on the tombola – won nothing – visited Beti's floral cream tea stall – ran away from Beti – and had just begun listening to the band when she heard a wave of commotion behind her: gasps and cries. Rowan spun around but it took several moments for the scene to sink in, to make sense, and even then: it made no sense.

People were floating. Not many . . . two, three . . . but even as Rowan was looking, another one went up . . . rising into the air. Not high but definitely not on the ground either. The floating people seemed entirely happy with their situation, serene smiles painted on their faces, while those left on the ground stared on, frozen in confusion and shock. There was a moment of dazed quiet and then, as another woman lifted off, panic erupted. People began to run, to scream, to flap and fluster and try to drag the floatees back to the ground.

Rowan staggered back. It made no sense. Had she not pulled Aslyn far enough away? Had his dreams somehow broken through? Had he managed to overpower the valerian?

Even as her mind raced, a stone dropped through the clouds of her thoughts with a thud of horrifying realization. The look on the people's faces as they floated up . . . she knew that look. She'd seen it before. Llewleyn's cloud cap mushrooms . . .

'Maiden, mother, and . . . oh, shit.'

This wasn't dream magic! It was her! She'd been in charge of chopping the mushrooms for the filling. She thought she'd checked the labels on the Tupperware . . . but there were so many mushrooms in the fridge . . . it was possible she'd chopped up the wrong batch.

She ran through the flailing crowd until she spotted Llewelyn. He was attempting to pull someone back to the ground by the ankle but they kept buoying back up like a helium balloon.

'LLEWELYN!' Rowan cried. 'I think I might have used the wrong mushrooms in the pies!'

'Well, I can see that, Rowan.'

'Oh Goddess! It's all my fault! I've ruined everything! I've ruined the fete! Winnie—'

'Hey,' he said, letting go of the ankle. The person floated off. 'We don't know it was your fault. Maybe I didn't label the tubs correctly—'

'I think we both know that's not true.'

'Don't worry, I'll take care of Winnie and we'll get this sorted quickly. There are enough witches here . . .' He frowned as the entire family behind Rowan rose into the air. 'I think it's best if you just go home.'

'Are you sure I can't help?'

'I think you've probably done enough.'

Rowan nodded and backed away. 'I'll go and pack up the pies at least.'

She made for their stall through the eruption of noise, the chaos of the crowds. It was empty now – she couldn't see any sign of Winnie, only Emlyn bobbing happily to one side of it, munching another pie. A hand landed on her arm. She turned to find Gareth.

'We didn't stop them!' he cried, pointing explosively around the fete. 'People are flying. Flying!'

'Actually . . .' Rowan bit her cheek. 'This is my bad. I might have mixed up the mushroom pie fillings with some particularly magical mushrooms.'

Gareth looked at her, eyes squinting seriously in the sun, and then – he burst into laughter. He doubled forwards and tried to catch his breath. 'This – was – you!'

'Gareth!'

'It's just – just – you went to all that trouble to stop Laila and Aslyn and then accidentally set half the fete afloat!'

'I'm sorry, HOW is this funny?' Rowan wailed. 'I've messed everything up! As always. Why is this the story of my entire life?' She hung her head. 'So much for my magic being spectacular . . .'

'Hey.' Gareth caught her eyes. 'This is not your story. Come on. I've got an idea.'

Rowan didn't entirely know why but she followed him. 'Where are we going?'

'You'll see.'

They ended up at the back of the field, in front of the hot-air balloon. Gareth nodded at it. 'Let's go for a ride.'

'WHAT?' Rowan shook her head. She glanced behind her

at the commotion of the fete. 'I don't know if you've noticed but I've probably done enough damage already.'

'Exactly. Everyone is going to be distracted for a while. May as well make the most of the chaos.' He stepped into the basket.

'I thought you were the sensible one . . .'

'What gave you that idea?' He grinned. 'I'm just not as stupid as Aslyn and Laila.'

Rowan looked back and forth between him and the hot-air balloon.

'Come on, we'll be back before anyone notices.' He extended a hand towards her.

Her head was still shaking but she took it. 'What the bloody Holle! I guess I've got nothing to lose.'

'That's the spirit,' he said, helping her up and closing the door of the basket. He loosened the rope. Within moments they began to rise up. Higher than the floating people. Higher than the tree tops. Gareth undid the rope and now there was nothing to stop them – nothing but the sky above. Rowan clutched the side of the basket. 'We're flying!' she cried. 'Wait, do you know how to fly this thing?'

'Not entirely, but we've got the wind and our magic. I don't think it'll be much harder than flying a kite . . .'

Rowan covered her eyes and laughed. 'Goddess above and below, what am I doing?' She peeked through her hands and could see the fete beneath them, no more than a distant flurry of activity. 'And what have I done? Winnie is going to be so stressed.'

'They'll sort it out. Magical cover-ups happen all the time,' said Gareth. 'At least no one's hurt. If anything, the floating people looked very happy. High as kites I think is the term.'

Rowan couldn't help laughing. Slowly, she removed her hands from her eyes. Coedyllaeth had opened up below them – its buildings and streets looking like a toy town from up here; a dream town huddled in a quilt of hills. Rowan realized she wasn't scared. The gentle drift of the hot-air balloon was strangely calming, the sky above beckoning blue. She closed her eyes, feeling the wind rush around her as if she was the kite now. Lost and free.

'Screw paragliding,' she whispered.

'What?' said Gareth, coming to stand next to her. He breathed in the air.

'Don't worry.'

He smiled, looking freer than Rowan had ever seen him, red hair blazing in the sun. 'It's pretty awesome, isn't it?'

'It is.' Rowan could barely believe it was happening. She turned to Gareth. 'Thank you for the perspective.'

'Happy to help. Look.' He pointed down. 'The stones on the hill.'

They looked as small as scattered seeds from their height but as they passed over them Rowan was sure she could feel the glimmer of their power lifting them higher.

'I bet Laila and Aslyn will find this all hilarious, at my expense . . .' Rowan muttered.

'Right now, who cares what they think.'

'I don't. It's just – I thought Laila liked me, but she was making a fool of me all that time with her stories and theories.'

'It wasn't about you. That's just Laila. Only half of what she says is true and the other half is questionable. She's always been that way, although it's got worse . . . She – she struggles with her mood and I think she uses her stories, her wild fantasies, to keep herself tethered. She doesn't mean to cause harm but she gets carried away.'

Rowan let Gareth's words settle. 'I didn't know she was struggling . . .'

'She doesn't really let people see the real her. The person beneath the moon-truth, as she would say. You should go see her. Say goodbye.'

'Maybe.' Rowan sighed.

'What about Aslyn?' He raised his eyebrows.

'I don't think I'll be talking to Aslyn again . . . I completely embarrassed myself in front of him. Told him I liked him. Was resoundingly rejected. And I'm not even sure I do like him, he's kind of—'

'An ass?'

'Yeah.' Rowan laughed. 'But a pretty one and I'm a sucker for the pretty ones.'

'I know how that feels,' said Gareth.

Rowan looked up at him. They were standing side by side, hands on the basket. For a moment, she'd forgotten they were flying hundreds of feet in the air. It felt easy, up here with him, lost in the wind. She hadn't noticed the colour of his eyes before – sky blue.

'Could I kiss you?' It slipped out before she could catch the words and stuff them back inside. Gareth froze. Rowan put her hands over her eyes. 'There we go again. Apparently I'm on a roll. Can we forget I said that? Can we forget that I have ever said anything ever?'

Gareth pulled her hands from her eyes. 'Rowan, I'm gay.'

'Oh—' His words sank in and the final pieces fell into place. 'You like Aslyn, don't you?'

He looked away. 'I did. A lot, for a long time, but . . . he's not been a great friend.'

'Did you tell him that you liked him?'

Gareth shook his head. 'He's not gay and I don't think he'd be into me even if he was. Thinks he's too good for the likes of me.'

'Then he can't see what's right in front of him.'

'Doesn't matter.' Gareth looked out over the unfolding hills. 'I'm getting over it, or trying to. I probably won't see him again after this summer anyway . . .'

'You should go see him. Say goodbye.'

Gareth grinned. 'Maybe.'

'Sorry for the whole kiss thing,' said Rowan. 'It's just, I was determined to kiss someone this summer. Ridiculous, I know. It's not like a kiss is going to change anything. I just wanted to know what it felt like . . . wanted someone to look at me that way . . . and then I'm thousands of feet in the air in a magically driven hot-air balloon after turning a whole town upside down, and you're really great, and suddenly a kiss didn't feel quite so impossible. Plus, it might be my only chance. Once we get back to school, I'll just be Rowan again. In fact, I'll be Rowan forever, which doesn't bode well for my kissing success. Also, we might die, because I'm not sure either of us knows how to land this thing—'

Gareth leant forwards and kissed her.

It only lasted a few seconds, but when it was over, Rowan touched her lips, shocked. 'You kissed me! Was it just to stop me talking?'

'Partly.' Gareth chuckled. 'But also, because your first kiss ought to be a memorable one, even if we have absolutely no future together . . .'

Rowan laughed, taking in the view below them. 'Well, I can safely say, I will never, ever forget this.'

'Rowan.'

'Yes?'

'What *are* you wearing on your head?'

'Oh, that.' She'd forgotten the hat was there. 'It's my Hedge Witch hat.'

'What does that mean?'

'It means that I've decided not to care so much about what people think of me.'

'Sounds like a good plan.'

'I intend to grow into it.'

She took it off and let the wind flow through her hair, breathing in the expanse of sky until her head was full of it.

The earth felt endless below them, hills rippling into the horizons, puddles of woodland, pocket-sized fields and the hedgerows – so many hedgerows. A network. Threads. Dividing the land. Stitching the land. *Edges*.

From above, Rowan could finally see what lay beyond them. *Magic*.

Turn over to discover more of the magical world
of *Hedgewitch* with Cari Thomas's
bestselling debut novel *Threadneedle*.

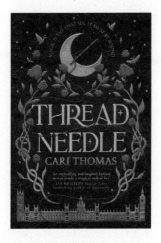

The bells rang out as they had done for hundreds of years, their sombre music sweeping over London with grace and stillness, bright as the moon which was full and ripe in the sky. Despite the late hour, the city below was restless, tossing and turning in the darkness with lights and buses and cars and people – everywhere people – walking, rushing, working, drinking, dancing, sleeping; none taking any notice of the bells at all.

Within the tower, the sound was deafening. Yet the women did not flinch as they stepped closer, forming a circle, their feet bare on the cold stone floor and their hair loose against plain robes. They pulled back their hoods, feeling the vibrations of the bells in their bones; feeling the buzz and blur of the city below; feeling the silence of the moon through the windows; feeling the languages of their own magic rising. The last chime rang out with finality.

Midnight. It was time.

They raised their arms to the sky.

They did not scream when it happened – the Seven were not made for such expressions, but even so they did not have time to scream. They possessed infinite years at their fingertips but not a moment of warning when it came—

The glass of the windows shattered. The night bled in. Words were spoken: impermeable and unbreakable. The women were yanked backwards, bare feet dragged along the floor. They were raised into the air, robes flaring, limbs frozen in the moonlight. All they could feel now was futility – the deep knowing that there was nothing they could do as the ropes wound around their necks and they dropped into the empty night.

Only then, as their bodies ceased to belong to them, did they do what any bodies would do: squirm and jerk and gargle and choke – slowly die.

Below, London carried on as before but the bells of Big Ben had never been so silent.

JOY

The neighbourhood was much like any other in the suburbs of London: straight-backed terraced houses, tall and narrow, abrupt faces, neat gardens, iron gates – closed now. Curtains were drawn and windows glowed against the darkness outside. It was quiet – only the distant jangle of traffic, footsteps carrying someone home, a dog barking, the whisper of trees in the wind – but one house was quieter than all the others.

Silent.

A silence so deep and still it went unnoticed, just like the house itself. Nobody turned to it as they walked by. The house was but a passing shiver – not a stone out of place on its gravel pathway, its porch primly adorned with hanging baskets, its white front door closed to the world beyond. Nothing stirred. Even the wind seemed to die at the door.

Not a sound could be heard from beyond its walls and yet inside, in the living room, a piano was playing of its own accord – the melody so fragile and heart-achingly beautiful it seemed to be made of silence itself. It fluttered against the windows but, not being able to escape, turned in on itself, disappearing into the emptiness between each note.

Seated in an armchair, a woman drifted her hands along to the music. Upon the floor, a girl had her eyes closed as if lost in it entirely, but her hand was clenched around a piece of knotted cord. She could not listen to the music. She could hear it, but she could not listen to it. Her knuckles were white.

The music slowed and a single note rang out, like a bell, pure and true and full of feeling.

The girl could take it no longer. She let a little of the sound through her defences, breathing in the joy of it. She gasped as the music began to fill her lungs. She grabbed at her throat, trying to breathe, but the air was too thick, too heavy with music – drowning her.

The woman's hands continued to flutter through the air.

The girl pulled one of the knots in her cord tighter. Tighter. She tried to wade against the panic, removing the music from her body, her mind. She pulled the knot so tight her fingers screamed. The joy in her heart silenced itself abruptly. The music washed against her but went no deeper. She took a tentative breath—

Relieved only for a second, she quickly tightened her eyes, clenched the cord and hardened herself. The song continued, beautiful no more, just a sound, an interesting arrangement of vibrations in the air. Not music.

It grew dark outside. The girl drowned again, and again, and again. Eventually the woman ceased to move her hands. The music stopped.

'Magic is the first sin; we must bear it silently,' said the woman, making the disappointment in her voice plainly heard.

'Magic is the first sin; we must bear it silently,' the girl responded.

'Go to bed, Anna.'

The girl was too tired to reply. She stood up, kissed her aunt goodnight on a cold, turned-away cheek and went upstairs.

The woman continued to sit in the armchair, thoughts turning slowly and heavy as the wheel of a mill. Soon it would be the girl's birthday. Would she be ready when the time came? She had to be ready. She moved her hands in the air and the piano began again.

She was pleased to find nothing but silence in her heart.